C000219157

The Path

By Robert H Wilde
Storyteller at CluedUpp Games

Foreword

Welcome to the world of CluedUpp Games, the creators of thrilling outdoor murder mystery events that have captivated millions of eager investigators around the globe.

CluedUpp Games has now ventured into the realm of more traditional storytelling, bringing you their first gamebook.

With a passion for engaging narratives and a dedication to the art of mystery-solving, CluedUpp Games invites you to step into the shoes of the Inspector and embark on an unforgettable journey.

As you navigate the pages of this unique book, you'll experience the same excitement, suspense, and uncertainty that have made CluedUpp's outdoor events a global sensation.

This gamebook is authored by Robert H. Wilde, our in-house scriptwriter, and game builder. Outside of work Robert is an historian, and respected author, publishing the British crime thriller series The Morthern Detectives, and True Crime Dossiers, amongst many others.

Enjoy the challenge and excitement that only CluedUpp Games can deliver, as you delve into this groundbreaking Be A Detective gamebook.

Introductions and Instructions

This is not a normal detective story. Someone has been killed, but YOU are the inspector leading the investigation, and the choices you make will decide how the case progresses and whether, in the end, YOU can catch the killer. You will frequently be up against the clock and faced with avenues to explore that will earn you relevant information, but also provide red herrings.

Do not read this book in page order. The book is divided into three hundred numbered sections. When you finish a section, you will be given choices, which will ask you to turn to the next section of your story. You will start at section one and go back and forth throughout the book until, if you succeed, you will finish at section 300. If you return to a section you've been to before, please skip to the options and select another one.

At one point in the book, you will be asked to start logging time spent. Ignore this rule for now, until you find it in the story, but it's included here for reference.

New Rules: for you, Inspector, the clock has started ticking. From now on certain sections will ask you to mark off five minutes. Keep track in the chart at the back of the book, and when you would tick off a time which asks you to turn to a section, turn immediately to that section. You may return to the line of enquiry you were looking at, that prompted the five minutes, later for free.

The chart is at the back of the book. You are against the clock: key events will trigger after a set amount of in-game time, and your investigation will end when you run out of time. Then you'll then be asked to name your suspect. You will not have time to explore everything, but equally, if you deduce a suspect early, you'll need to keep spending time to reach the end trigger. You win if you deduce the killer and their motive, but to achieve a maximum score you will need several playthroughs to find all the secrets.

Good luck Inspector.

As you step out of your car a building towers above you. It's brick and glass, smooth lines, nothing like the brutalist seventies concrete of the headquarters you started your career in and which your younger colleagues regard the same way you treat a Norman castle. You cross the car park with ease as you're in early as usual, passing through reception without needing to wave your ID. As you turn a corner you avoid a coffee machine no one ever uses in favour of many a run to the café on the corner and come to your office. The base of the Serious Crimes Unit, on the second floor of the county's police headquarters, and a place you've called home for over a decade.

"Morning Inspector," a woman calls out, and you look over to see Detective Constable Laura Stewart staring at a whiteboard. Everyone has their way of thinking about a case, from re-reading interviews over and over again to walking the location until you've got every inch in your head, but DC Stewart just liked to stand and stare at the whiteboards like someone waiting for their partner to come back after a particularly stormy day at sea. Still, it worked, and that's why Stewart had been your closest colleague for the last three years. Suit always immaculate, face capable of being coldly inscrutable or charmingly irreverent, Stewart comes over and looks for the coffee you always bring her.

There's no coffee today.

"Everything alright Inspector?" she asks you, her voice rising with a mixture of excitement and shame at the latter.

"Got a call just as I was parking up," you explain, "uniform is attending a call in from a jogger…"

You leave the sentence unfinished. Joggers only ever rang in just after dawn for one reason, and today was another example.

"A body..."

You nod. A body had been found, and there was no coffee as you'd pick some up on the way to the scene.

Turn to Section 27.

2

You ask, "And what, Mr Hewitt, does the puzzle mean to you?"

"I'm sorry, what?" He seems startled.

"You're clearly a dedicated follower..."

"Traveller."

"...traveller, very keen to complete The Path. Would what it mean to you to finish it?"

Hewitt seems to be trying to stare you down, and he pins you with his eyes. His mind isn't working, you can see he has one view and one view only, which comes out with an almost snarl. "Everything." His eyes fill with his visions of the world post his success.

"Go on?"

"We are all dedicated but I am more dedicated than the rest. To not solve it now... that would be a failure. No one wants to be a failure. But I will not fail. I will simply complete the puzzle because I'm a great puzzling mind, it's simply just something I can and will do. Everyone else can grind away, and when I announce the victory... it will be glorious."

"In a way, you must like the puzzle, and Blanc?" You honestly don't know what he'll say to that.

"No. It's a vehicle. But I must complete it first."

Go back to section 231 to continue questioning.

3

"So what's this about a letter?" you ask Robertson.
"I'd hold you up an evidence bag, but it's already gone to forensics for a look, so instead I have this photo of it..." and she points to your computer screen. You bend down and take a look as she explains, "It arrived in the post this morning. An actual letter, in the actual Royal Mail post, like something from the past. I think you'll be able to see why it was brought to our attention.

"To The Police,

There are those of us who walk the Path. Reginald Forrest has given us a superb mystery to solve. But you now walk your own path, because I have given you a mystery to solve. I will not tolerate anyone else completing it, I will become the Panda's Paw and strike down anyone who gets ahead of me. Can you walk your path and find me, before I walk the Path and find the Panda? There will be others, oh God yes, there will be others. But how many is up to you, police. You will hear more from me. My word is out there, online. The Panda's Paw."

You stand up from the screen and scratch your nose. "What do you think?" Robertson asks you.

- To reply, "This isn't from the killer" and investigate elsewhere, turn to section 88.
- To refocus the investigation into any evidence from the letter, add five minutes and turn to section 119.

8

You ask Greg, "I assume you'd heard about Mr Webb's murder before you got the call asking you to be here?"

"Yeah, I saw it on the news, and I knew it was him. Instant. I thought fuck, who's he pissed off, cos he wasn't the type to ever kill himself, far too full of himself for that, so yeah, I knew he'd done it. When you gave me the call, wasn't surprised. Know you'd be doing your job, following leads. Man speaks to group about hundred grand prize, dies soon after, yeah, yeah, that'd do it."

"And what do you think about the murder?"

"Someone's done us all a fucking favour, haven't they. Man's an arse, and now he's, what's that Shakespeare phrase, hoist by his own petard. Live like an annoying bastard, get swatted for it."

"So you're happy he's dead?"

"Yeah."

"And you don't think that's an overreaction?"

"Everything is these days. No middle ground. Just crazy shit. But why do you reckon it's to do with The Path? That's what I wanna know. Webb, he's a fucking prick, he's bound to have pissed loads of people back off in your patch. No jealous exes? Mad girlfriends? Bad boyfriends? Stuck it where he shouldn't? Dunno what you think we've got to do with it."

Turn to section 161.

"Have you formed any ideas about what's been happening?" you ask Hewitt.

"Yes, yes, I have. If someone was killing people on the Path, then you should be protecting those of us in the Cartel, not questioning us like we're killers. If I thought there was a connection, I'd be taking security provisions. But this is what I think. Serial killers are big business. Catch a serial killer and you'll get a book deal, have an ITV prime-time show made about you, you'll finish your own version of the Path. So my conclusion is you're desperate for all this to be linked. Now, the moment you can prove it, then I expect a policeman in my house guarding me, and the other three too. But until that happens, I'm of the mind you're chasing your own promotion Inspector. I mean really, a serial killer for a puzzle game?"

To ask, 'Did you know Gareth Hyax?' turn to section 232.
To ask where they were at the time of Hyax's murder, turn to section 102.
To ask if they know anyone angry at Hyax, turn to section 36.
To leave Hewitt, return to section 129.

⸙ 6

"Do you know if anyone was angry at Mr Webb?" you ask Krasinski.
She spits out a surprised laugh and says, "Yes!"
"Who?"
"Well someone, they killed him!"
You don't laugh, just nod and continue, "But in your dealings with him, was anyone angry at him?"
"I don't know of anyone I'd say angry... I mean the travellers are all a fairly highly strung bunch and there's plenty of heated discussions about minute details, and that's one benefit of being by yourself on quiz shows,

there's ultimately no one to tell you off, just you and millions of people if you check Twitter. I don't check Twitter."

"If we could stick to the investigation?"

"Oh right, well there's lots of angry people on the Path, but it's all jealousy. I don't think anyone would ever threaten anyone. I mean he did end up in a shouting match when he was here, but no harm came to it, just two men getting their dicks, sorry, penises bruised."

"Oh?"

"Yes, Glen got very riled up by his tone and ended up shouting at him, before he, err, Glen stormed off. Webb left shortly after, and I doubt he and Glen have spoken much since."

Turn to section 270.

You have a sad task to do. Specialist officers visit and tell Wright's husband that she has been killed, and work to calm him, and help him adjust and grieve. Then you have to question him.

"I appreciate your time," you tell him, "but if you can answer a few questions, it will help us."

"Anything, anything," he says half choking back tears.

"Phyllis rang me, asking to speak urgently. Do you know why?"

"No, not a clue. My wife... she didn't say a thing about needing the police. Nothing."

"There's nothing she's said recently that felt odd?"

"She follows her oath, she never gossips about her work, but if she felt threatened, or if something was going wrong, she would tell me. I'm sorry officer, but I honestly don't have a clue why this has happened."

"That's okay sir. Thanks for your time. One last thing, do you have any pets?"

"No, no we don't, never have."

To wait and speak to the scene of crime team about their findings, turn to section 222.

To search Phyllis' office, turn to section 235.

To move on the investigation, turn to section 46.

8

"Sorry?" Hewitt asks.

"The security cameras at your shop," Robertson says turning to him, "they're broken. I asked your staff to download the footage from the last two days, and when they went over, they could see the system was down and not doing anything."

"How odd," Hewitt replies.

"You didn't know?" you ask him.

"Well it's CCTV, you only check it when something's gone wrong. We caught a shoplifter on it last week, so it must have broken since then. Maybe we didn't restart it properly."

"I see," you reply.

"But you'll see me in the shop every night working, that night was no different. Maybe something outside has caught me, on the route home, that sort of thing."

"Thank you," you say making a note.

"I do hope this won't count against me."

"I'll be honest," you begin, "it's a bigger issue than if you'd been taped sat there."

"I quite understand. I had better get it working again soon, did you," and he turns to Robertson, "tell my assistant to put a call in to the engineer and get it fixed?"
"No."
"Then I had better do that. We don't want anyone else walking out with stock."

Turn to section 231 to continue.

9

"Did you know Phyllis Wright?"
Caroline sticks her tongue in the side of her mouth and thinks. "I didn't know her personally, no, we never spoke or anything like that."
"But you did know of her?"
"Yes, yes, I did. Some of the chaps from the Cartel have mentioned her. I think some of them have actually spoken to her, as in patient spoken, but I figured that was all personal information and didn't try to remember any of it. When you're filling your head up with quiz answers you don't bother with who your friend is telling all their personal life too."
"Can you try and think and be more specific?"
"Maybe I can't pick any because they all have. Yes, I'm going to go with 'like they all have' as my answer."

To ask what they were doing at the time of the murder / arson, turn to section 296.
To ask if they knew any connection between Phyllis and The Path, turn to section 146.
To ask if they have any further ideas on the case, turn to section 26.
Or return to section 218.

13

"Mr Weald, as you might be aware a man called Harold Webb was recently killed. Did you know this man, and how?"

"Bit of a leading question there," Jay replies to you, "seeing as you know full well, I knew him. He was a 'blogger', and he came to a meeting of the Catan Cartel."

"You sounded upset by the term blogger there?"

"Yes, I am. What is a blogger? They are rarely, if ever, properly edited and proofread. At least a journalist tends to have their work checked. The internet has given an entire layer of amateurs a veneer of respectability while people like myself, editors, are being frozen out, pay being cut, because no one uses us and expectations are radically reduced. So excuse my scepticism at calling Webb anything other than a simple fanzine creator."

"Point noted," you tell him, "however, to return to the matter at hand, you can confirm you've met Mr Webb."

"Yes, he did come to the meeting, and I was there. The meeting had only five people, Mr Webb, and every one of the others is sat in this room with us."

"Thank you for confirming that."

Turn to section 210.

You ring the bell of a white plastic door and take a step back. After a few seconds you can hear movement, and the door opens to reveal a man who's clearly the worse for wear: unshaven, stained t-shirt, bags under his eyes.

He looks at you as if he'd just been staring at a screen for six straight hours.

"Yeah?"

"Hello, I'm from the police and I'd like to ask you some questions."

"No," he replies.

"No?"

"Not getting anything out of me without a lawyer."

"Mr Cook, you are under arrest. You do not have to say anything, but it may harm your defence if you do not mention when questioned something which you later rely on in court. Anything..." You don't get any further because Cook has run off, back into his house, slamming his door shut, so you calmly walk round the back off the house, down the open side passage of the terrace, and find Cook face down on the ground where Robertson has wrestled him after waiting by the back door. You help cuff him and assist in his journey to a police car for a trip to the station.

Turn to section 150.

◊ 12

You've popped out to the café and grabbed a pair of large coffees and two of their ham and mustard toasties, then knocked on the door of Keith. He works in headquarters and, like Pele was known by one name because he was a legendary footballer, Keith was simply known as that because he was exceptionally good at technology even if he looked like he'd just been electrocuted by it.

"Hi there!" he greets you, all waving arms and leaping out of his chair, and he hungrily takes a coffee, a toastie, and then he grins widely as he takes a phone from you. Still in an evidence bag, tested for prints and DNA, it's the phone that was found in Harold Webb's car, the man evidently having rushed out so fast he hadn't taken it...or had he been asked to leave it behind?

Keith turns it on and nods sagely to himself as he sees the lock screen. Evidently this and the simple dimensions of the phone have told Keith what he needs, and he drops down to his desk and starts connecting the phone up. You eat a toastie as Keith makes a series of hmms and ahs, before he taps a monitor to his right.

"Here you go, all the calls and texts and what have you. Shall we see what we've got?"

You take a seat, pick up your drink, and you both begin to look.

Harold Webb did not appear to be that interested in other people. He had names in his phonebook yes, but the call logs, the text logs, and the messaging services revealed his main contact was his parents' home line, many times a day. The only other contact of note was a WhatsApp chat group for GWA, Gamers With Attitude, which Harold was in but taking less and less of a role in conversation. There was nothing that could not be explained, GWA excepted. If you were hoping the killer had arranged the meetup by text, it hadn't happened.

"Thanks Keith," you tell him, "if you can send the data to my team..." You go and speak to the obvious next candidates: The GWA.

Turn to section 83.

13

"Sorry, did you just say confession?" you blurt out to Robertson.

16

"Yes, this is going to sound very odd, but 999 had a call from someone who wanted the police to visit him because he wanted to confess to a series of murders, including Mr Hyax..."

"Just... rang into the room?"

"Yep."

"How odd. Who's gone?"

"Phone call's just come through, I thought we both had better go?"

"Right on to it," you reply, and you both rush down to the car park, get into Robertson's car and you're back being driven through a city that is both strange and familiar. You find yourself being driven up hills so steep your calves hurt in sympathy, and parking outside a line of tall, terraced houses in a very narrow road.

"This is one of the poorest areas of Sheffield," Robertson tells you as you both get out. "So keep an eye out of the windows on the car."

"That bad?"

"Well, we tell the students not to come here alone. They come here to buy drugs, and saying don't do that didn't work so now we just encourage a mob of them."

Turn to section 80 to knock on the door.

14

"Would you say the main issue among the Cartel at the moment is The Path?" you ask Krasinski. She nods almost violently.

"We've tackled a lot of puzzles over the years we've been together..."

"How long is that?"

"...ten years. Some we've pursued ourselves, some we've pursued in competition, but nothing has grabbed all of us quite like The Path."

"How would you describe it?"

"Oooh, it's something which intrigues the mind, because you have the riddles and the text passages, all of which are really puzzles, but it intrigues the eyes, because you're also cross-referencing the imagery."

"Which is..."

"No original artwork was commissioned for The Path. I'd thought of speaking to the artists but it's all work which has been cleverly sourced and re-used, I suppose you could say. Also Gato Blanc took photographs himself, which is one reason why Sheffield has been suggested as a possible final resting place."

"You don't think starting a global mystery and hiding the answer next door to you is a little lacking?" you ask.

"No, no," and Krasinski leaps to Gato's defence. "The man is a puzzle master, a professor. To read his work is to face, and solve, genius. I'm sure the perfect answer happened to be local."

Turn to section 118.

Turn to section 118.

⟍ 15

Robertson turns the car into the parking area of a coffee shop. As you get out you can see Mrs Forrest already waiting inside for you. You rang her and asked to meet, then she asked if she could do it privately as she might not want her husband to hear. She looks nervous as you enter, buy a coffee, and come and sit down with her.

"Mrs Forrest."

"Inspector. What is it?"

"How do you know Gareth Hyax?"

"Oh Gareth? He runs Puzzle! It's one of the leading puzzle magazines and he's given The Path a lot of coverage. In fact he told me Path-centric issues are his best sellers and..." She slows, a sudden realisation dawning. "You know don't you, that's why you're here and not around my husband."

"Would you like to be honest with us?" you ask her.

She takes a deep breath and begins. "Gareth is fighting a cutthroat battle with his competitors. The puzzle market isn't big enough for them anymore, and in order to get the edge and get the subscribers, he's determined to solve The Path. By solve I mean he approached me with a large sum of money to sell him the answer. And... the only reason I didn't agree, given our parlous financial state, was because I was angling for more. I guess he's reported me for fraud or something?"

"I'm afraid to tell you, Mrs Forrest, that Gareth Hyax has been murdered."

She instantly retches, grabs the table and calms herself. "By the same man? Person, whatever."

"That's a working hypothesis, yes."

Turn to section 190.

16

"Where were you when Phyllis was murdered?" you ask him.

Jay looks at you, clearly thinking and taking a decision. Then he speaks quickly as if a dam has broken. "Fuck it, fuck it, I might as well say. I was here, drunk, on the floor, hating myself. You see Inspector, I haven't been able to do my own writing for weeks. I can proofread, I can edit, but when I try to work for myself, I dry up and do nothing. Phyllis had been trying with me, but nothing worked, and you've been in the kitchen, you know I've started drinking to block it all out. So I've no alibi, I was just here getting shitfaced from my own failure. And while I did that Phyllis was killed. Maybe I am, in some small way, to blame for it all. Karmically."

To ask if he knew Phyllis Wright, turn to section 288.
To ask if they knew any connection between Phyllis and The Path, turn to section 86.
To ask if they have any further ideas on the case, turn to section 110.
Or return to section 46.

To ask if he knew Phyllis Wright, turn to section 288.
To ask if they knew any connection between Phyllis and The Path, turn to section 86.
To ask if they have any further ideas on the case, turn to section 110.
Or return to section 46.

⁊ 17

"Have you had much contact with the readers? How has The Path been received?"

Forrest licks his lips and replies, "The book has sold very well, and I know there's lot of people dedicating an awful lot of time and energy on solving it. No one has yet. However, that passion has problems. At first, I played the Gato character online in forums and spoke to people, but I've backed off from that. I still talk to our local gaming group who have gone after it full-bodied, the Catan Cartel, but aside from them I try and step back. The problem is the letters."

"I understand. I saw your wife come in with post..."

Mrs Forrest explains, "We don't have any delivered to the house. The local newsagent takes it in for me, then I go and collect it and screen it, so no trouble follows us back here."

"Okay, but you've had harassing letters..."

"Yes, yes, I had this one only today," and she waves one at you.

"Would you be willing to show us these letters? Let us take them for analysis?"

"Yes, sure."

You lean back and think to yourself, if Mrs Forrest screens the letters, and she's bringing back the threatening ones, what exactly is she leaving at the newsagents.

Add the Keyword LETTERS, which will be available to you when you return to the station.

To visit the newsagent for yourself, add five minutes and turn to section 297.

To return to headquarters, turn to section 75.

⸱18

Baxter opens his door, but he doesn't say hello, he just disappears into his lounge. You follow him, and find him sitting down stroking Coco, who regards you like she might a mouse, and you might a criminal.

"Thank you for agreeing to speak to us," you say to Baxter.

"Is this going to happen every time someone is murdered?" he asks agitated. "Will these questions never end."

"We hope to find the killer soon, but any insight you can give us is appreciated."

"Well," he begins in reply to you, "I appreciate you consider me a criminal psychologist of great renown, but I fear you'll be disappointed. Caroline would be far more useful to you. She's trying to solve it. Maybe she'll beat

21

you and you'll have to appear on the news and explain
your failure."

To ask if he knew Phyllis Wright, turn to section 213.
To ask what they were doing at the time of the murder /
arson, turn to section 255.
To ask if they knew any connection between Phyllis and
The Path, turn to section 125.
To ask if they have any further ideas on the case, turn to
section 63.
Or return to section 218.

19

"Mr Helsh..."
"Greg, please, yeah."
"Greg, did you know Mr Webb?"
"Yeah, I did. Yeah. Yeah. Err... you want me to say how, or
talk about him, or what?"
"What would you say your contact with him was?"
"I knew his blog, right, and I read his blog, and socials
because he follows The Path, but can I get in any trouble
for this?" He still looks nervous.
"You can't get into trouble for giving us your assessment
of a man."
"Yeah, good. So I knew of his blog, and I thought it would
be good to invite him to come and speak to us. Yunno, we
ask him questions and he asks us questions, a bit of
networking, thought it would be a cool thing to do. But I
regret it. Yeah, I regret it, cos he was a horrible man. He
came to my house before the meeting, so I could take
him, and he was rude, rude to me in my own house, but I
gritted my teeth and I brought him along, but he was

rude to all of us, just an unpleasant man and I wish he'd
not come into my life."

Turn to section 298.

20

You arrive at Greg Helsh's listed address. It's a large
suburban house, but something is obviously wrong. The
front lawn is very overgrown, borders full of shrubs were
once clearly cared for and now run wild, and the bin
tucked round the side is full of empty alcohol bottles,
from lagers to spirits. Greg opens the door looking like a
man who's tried to have a shave in the time between you
arranging the meeting to now, and you find yourself
sitting in a lounge where the corners have had children's
toys swept into them and gathered dust, even though
there's no evidence of children actually being present
recently.
"What's up?" Greg asks you as he sinks into a chair. "If
you want a drink, err, a coffee or anything, you can help
yourself."

To ask did you know Gareth Hyax, turn to section 159.
To ask where they were at the time of Hyax's murder,
turn to section 244.
To ask if they know anyone angry at Hyax, turn to section
269.
To ask if Helsh has any ideas about the murder, turn to
section 127.
To leave Helsh, return to section 129.

As you head to reception to take a look at security, you pass a porter in the corridor and explain to him the situation. He asks to see your ID, and when that's presented, he leads you through a staff door and into the behind the scenes of the hotel. Down some stairs and next to the kitchen is the room where the cameras work from... and the porter opens the door, and you look inside. Unlike the far hotel from earlier, no one constantly monitors these cameras, instead the data is collected by hard drive and looked at if needed. The porter asks you to wait and disappears off, and shortly after a man in a sharp suit and no name tag appears, the manager. You explain the situation to him, and he sits right down and starts trying to use the software. It's frustrating for you to watch him flail, and frustrating to him to do it, but soon enough he has the camera that's closest to your room... whereupon you discover there is nothing aiming down the corridor including your door, it's all in the stairwells, lifts and exits. Whoever went into your room, there's no way to pick them out from the people on the cameras.

However, you lean in as the camera closest to you captures a figure moving swiftly through...

Turn to section 55.

22

"Where were you on the night of the murder?" you ask with a totally straight face, not expecting Hewitt to start openly laughing. "A private joke?"

"No, no," Hewitt replies, "but I've been waiting for you to say that. It's the most police question ever isn't it, where were you."

You tilt your head and say, "It was pretty magical to say it for the first time, yes."

"I bet."

"So, where were you?"

"Easy, same place I am every evening, in my pharmacy. I don't have a partner unless you count my gorgeous cat, I don't have kids, but what I do have is a thriving business I pay closer attention to. Every night I restock, stock take, do accounts, prepare prescriptions, so I don't know how much you know about chemists or shopkeeping in general, but I sit and sort it all out."

You nod, "And is there anyone who can corroborate that? Are there other staff members with you?"

"If there were they would demand payment. No, there are no humans there with me, but luckily everything is fully covered by closed-circuit television. I can ring," and he pulls out a mobile phone, "and get the footage secured for you?"

Turn to section 226.

Turn to section 226.

‹ **23**

You ask Krasinski, "I suppose you've pretty much answered this, but after Webb left the meeting did you have any more contact with him?"

"He gave us all his phone number, in case we wanted to continue the conversation, and I'll be honest I went home and stuck it straight in the bin. He knew nothing, no need to speak to him. I mean I guess the murder stops him being the first one to solve it, but he wasn't close..." a look of realisation passes over Krasinski's face, "unless he really was nearly there, and he hid details from us like we did to him. That's something for you to pursue."

"Indeed. So no further contact?"

"No, no, sorry, there was further contact."

"How so?"

"He messaged me! For a moment I was proud that he'd decided I was the one who'd be the most help to him, then it turned out he was just trying to chat me up. At least he didn't send a dick pic, but I suppose he flexed his puzzle cred. He said we'd be the most media-friendly couple going, given our respective fame. I soon stopped replying. I might be single but I'm not desperate."

Return to section 153 to pursue another line of questioning.

24

"Where were you at the time of Phyllis Wright's murder?" you ask Greg.

"I was in the pub. Yep, drinking, in the pub. Can't tell you much of what happened cos it's blurry, but I was definitely in it, and I know the landlord has cameras so it shouldn't be too much trouble to prove it. I'm thinking, Inspector, I'm thinking, if I hang out at places where there's cameras, then I have an alibi. Not stupid Old Greg."

You reply, "That does gently imply you know when the murders are happening."

"Does it? Oh bollocks. Yeah, well, it'll work this time, ring the Crossed Keys."

You decide to do just that and retreat into the garden and ring. The landlord answers quickly, and once you've explained the situation, he assures you he will personally vouch for Greg being in there, as he was a good customer "this time."

To ask if he knew Phyllis Wright, turn to section 246.
To ask if they knew any connection between Phyllis and The Path, turn to section 97.
To ask if they have any further ideas on the case, turn to section 273.
Or return to section 218.

⌄ 25

"Jay, in your dealings with Webb, did you learn of anyone, or believe anyone, to have reason to kill him?"
He holds his palms up and answers, "No, I don't know why anyone would kill anyone honestly."
"You're designing a game about a murder?"
"That's a game... it's not really happening. The game isn't a substitute for some repressed desire to kill someone. I just like solving them."
"Did you know of anyone who was angry with Webb?"
"That's more understandable, at least from my headspace. I suppose you could say we are all angry at Webb, because he's a rival traveller on the Path and he's already making money off his social media talking about it. I wouldn't be good in front of camera, but Webb's YouTube was racking up the views, and the income. I think we'd all like a piece of that. And yes, I know you expect me to say Greg was angry, and I guess Greg was angry, but honestly, Webb was a pathetic sort of man who'd come to probe us, and I'm glad Glen kicked him out."

You allow your surprise to show in a raised eyebrow. "Speaking of Greg…"

Turn to section 224.

26

"Do you have any further ideas on the case?"
"Yes," Caroline replies, and she holds up a cricket bat.
"It's something to do with sport?" you ask.
"No."
"It's something to do with wood or…"
"This is self-defence."
"What?"
"Think about it Inspector. Someone is killing people who have nearly solved The Path. Well, who are they going to feel threatened by very soon, if they haven't already? Moi! That killer is going to come for me, and I will be ready with my new doors and my bat, and I will repel all attackers, intruders, and invaders."
"You've got to be careful with that," you warn her.
"I think you'll find you can't stop me having a sporting implement. It's not like I'm waving a big sword at you. I'd like a gun ideally, but I don't live in the right country."

To ask if she knew Phyllis Wright, turn to section 9.
To ask what they were doing at the time of the murder / arson, turn to section 296.
To ask if they knew any connection between Phyllis and The Path, turn to section 146.
Or return to section 218.

You park your unmarked vehicle alongside a pair of fully marked police cars and say a silent thanks that the light rain has stayed away since dawn. You've pulled off a small road, down a track of well-worn gravel, and are now in a parking area surrounded on all sides by trees. The county has a number of woods which are large for Britain but tiny for Europe or the United States, and your target lies within one. As you step out on to the still wet ground, a black leather shoe squelching down stone, the uniformed officer who'd been waiting for you comes over. It's a young man, one of the newest intake, but he doesn't look green around the gills. He's trained for this; he's done this a lot before already.

He speaks as you and DC Stewart follow him along a dirt path into the wood. "Morning Inspector, Constable. We received a call at 6:16 this morning from a woman who had been jogging through the woods. She reported a body laying in a patch of weeds, plants, whatever the short stuff is called. We attended immediately and... yeah, she wasn't wrong. This path was clear before we started going up and down it. As for the others... Ah, here we are."

You turn a corner, and the path opens out on to a small clearing. There's three paths leading off in total, including the one you've just come down, and the clearing has a wooden bench on which a dead bundle of flowers slowly rots. However what attracts the attention is the man's corpse that's clearly been dropped down in the undergrowth. A pale, blue face stares up into the treetops, mouth open in shock. Near to the body are two more uniformed officers standing guard, checking.

You walk over, careful to only step in the areas identified as safe by uniform. You can already see footsteps left in the muddy ground from whatever happened here.

"What have you found?" you ask.

"We decided, given the weather, to take the jogger to the station and let her give a full statement there, but we've got the main details: she ran this path at 6:00 pm last night and it was clear, and ran it at 6:00 am this morning, as soon as the rain had stopped. That's when she found the body, so it's arrived overnight. Forensics are on their way, but I feel able to say there's evidence of multiple stab wounds."

You look the body up and down and nod in agreement. The victim was six foot tall, overweight in build, and wearing a hoodie of a band you've never heard of... not that you'd be able to tell much about the logo as the hoodie is full of holes where someone's stabbed the victim. Blood has stained the clothes and the plants. The victims hands were cut where he'd obviously tried to fight off the blade. Your conclusion is the victim was killed here and left, rather than brought along and dumped.

"Who is he?" you ask as you look at the cold face.

"We don't know," the PC replies. "There's no obvious identification on the body, if they had a wallet, it's not here."

"So theft a possibility?" Stewart asks.

"Could be," you reply, not wanting to rule anything out suddenly, "but he'd be damned unlucky to be robbed and murdered in the middle of this forest." You feel sure something far more complex is happening here. "Any timing on forensics arriving?"

"Should be ten minutes."

That gives you time to explore. "Any sign of the murder weapon?"

"Nothing, nothing but the body, but there's clear signs of travel along the other paths."

Take a closer look at the paths, turn to section 58.
Head down the left path, turn to section 160.
Head down the right path, turn to section 236.
Head down the path you came in on, turn to section 105.

⊿ 28

It's probably okay to admit it to yourself, you're missing Stewart, so in her honour you go and stand in front of the whiteboard. You've been given one for your investigation, although you've had to fill it in yourself which takes you back a few years. As you watch, you're brought a coffee by Robertson, and it's exactly the type you like. You're getting part of the station furniture! That makes you feel warm, which is good because after someone rifled through your possessions your view of Sheffield was starting to dim.
"See anything?" Robertson asks.
"Yeah, yeah actually I do," you say as something does jump out. "Caroline Krasinski, her alibi was fake, and we have a report on her sneaking about. Maybe at night, maybe at other times. I was wondering, we should have someone tail her, see where she's going, see if it's related. We need to rule out her activity. Are we able to get someone to follow her?"
As you finish you realise Robertson is grinning to herself.
"What is it?" you ask.
"Have a guess," she asks you.
"I'd rather you just told me..."

Turn to section 52 to find out.

"Anything else?" Krasinski asks.

"Yes, just following that up, can anyone corroborate what you just said?"

"About staying at home?"

"Yes, can anyone give you an alibi."

"Oh. No. I was just relaxing on my lonesome. I don't suppose a half drunk bottle of wine and the history of my cable provider is much of a help is it."

"I'm afraid not."

"In that case... oh dear I don't think there is any way I can prove that to you. Does this count against me? Does this make me a suspect? Oh, I'm going to be a suspect."

"No, it doesn't," you explain, "but as you say, it's a question we have to ask and it's helpful in establishing what's going on."

"Hmm. I hope you don't think I'm being lazy just sitting in on my own, I had to fill my head with puzzle answers so what better than to consume the soaps, because they get asked about, then some documentaries, bit of reading, all the information I fill my head with. And, of course, the time I spend researching The Path."

"But you didn't do anything with The Path that night?"

"No, I didn't."

You have gained the Keyword NIGHT. Make a note of it. Then turn to section 251 to ask more questions.

30

Caroline Krasinski is arrested by police as she is leaving her house. She claims she is on the way to school to put in some cover, but she is instead handcuffed and taken to the station. There is no sign of the knife, or the missing man.

It is only later that day, when Reginald Forrest's mutilated body is discovered, that it's confirmed you arrested the wrong person. You are taken off the case, and Sheffield's own police take charge, review the material you have collected, and arrest the right killer. You have failed Inspector.

To choose a different suspect return to section 242, or playthrough the book again and search for more clues.

To choose a different suspect return to section 242, or playthrough the book again and search for more clues.

⩔ 31

You leave the hotel and return to the scene of Hyax's murder. The body has been removed, and the area combed for clues. A final pair of SOCO officers are just making their last notes, so you go over to them.
"What have you found?" you ask.
"Frustrating. No recent prints or DNA, no obvious fibres but we'll go over the victim's clothes with a toothcomb obviously. The murder weapon was here, a common-or-garden kitchen knife, bent in the frenzy of the attack, cheap thing, but no prints. Someone's cleaned it, thing stinks of blood and bleach. We'll continue digging of course, but no breakthrough for you."
"I understand. Thanks for the hard work."
When you get back into Robertson's car, your phone beeps. There's a message from the team doing the post mortem.

"Full results coming in the morning Inspector, but felt you'd appreciate news. We performed our post mortem on Mr Hyax, then pulled up the post mortem on Mr Webb. Hyax hadn't had any breakfast, had a little alcohol left in his system from the night before, and suffered massive blood loss from repeated deep knife wounds. Afraid to say everything matches, the type of blows, the severity, the weapon used. I would not hesitate to say these are the same killer."

You reply, "Thanks."

Return to section 62.

32

You lean forward and ask, "You said facts 'we hadn't already come to'. Do you share your workings with the rest of the Cartel?"
"Never!" he spits loudly, then regains some calm. "What I mean is, we do not share anything or pool resources, until we know the others have found the same, and then we will jointly confer as the secret is already out. I must remind you, Inspector, that this is a great challenge with a huge prize and none of the Cartel wish to see the others get it. Friendly rivalry, but rivalry all the same.
"What are your views on the others in the Cartel?"
Hewitt sneers as he says, "They would quite possibly need the help of, but I do not. They're all good puzzlers, or they wouldn't fit into our group, but they are not good enough for this as evidenced by the fact they haven't solved it."
"But you haven't solved it..."

"..." Hewitt looks at you like a cat observes a mouse with a gun before spluttering, "It takes time. It is a big challenge. I have complete faith I will solve it."

To ask about the puzzle, turn to section 79.
For other questions, return to section 231.

⌐ 33

"We received a report only a few minutes ago," Robertson says to you as she passes you a piece of paper. "Traffic had a call of someone driving "weirdly," yep, they said weirdly, and we didn't get much more out of them about what that meant. But the key thing is the caller had written down the licence plate number... and you'll never guess whose it is."

"Go on..." Your mind has many possibilities in it, none of them good.

"The car is registered to Reginald Forrest, aka Gato Blanc, aka The Path's author."

"Has it been reported stolen?" you check.

"Nope."

"How very odd, yes, we better go and see if we can find him. Any sightings beyond that one?"

"No, we have the location, but you've assumed the gender there."

"Oh?"

"The caller was very specific, it might be Reggie's car, but there was a woman driving it..."

"Winnie? Reginald's wife?" you wonder out loud.

"Must be? We don't have a description beyond 'woman'. The witness was... vague."

"Let's go on to it."

To go to the area of the sighting, add five minutes and turn to section 93.

To use the CCTV to try and track Forrest's car, add five minutes and turn to section 152.

⏱ 34

Everything feels heavy and dark. You know there's something in the distance, but you just can't move to it, or even see it. Slowly the dark resolves and you feel the outline of your own head, and an aching in the middle of it. Slowly the outline of your head spreads, so you can feel a body, and your eyes, and you can recall you're the inspector, you have your eyes closed, and you're lying down...

As consciousness returns you open your eyes and find you aren't in a car park. Instead you're in a largely white and pale green room, and a beeping to one side reveals you're attached by the arm to monitoring devices.

"You're awake," says a voice to your left, and it hurts your head to turn and find DC Stewart sat there.

"What?"

"I came over as soon as we got the call. Someone found you laying in a hotel car park, wound on the back of the head. Not life threatening but it's going to keep you in bed for a few weeks while you recover."

"The case!"

"You're off the case. You're doing nothing for a while."

Inspector, your investigation ends here in failure, unless you return to section 109 and pick a different path.

"We're investigating the murder of a Mr Harold Webb. Did you know the victim?"

"Yes, I did." Krasinski finishes her reply and pauses for a moment, before adding "Oh... do you want me to talk about him?"

"Sorry, yes, please tell us what you know."

"Okay, this is my first time being interviewed by the police. Quite a rush I must say. Okay, Webb is, was, is, was a big name in the puzzle blogosphere. He has a considerable following among hardcore puzzlers, such as the kind you'll find in the Cartel, and in casuals, who make up the bulk of his views on YouTube and the like. I've never been tempted by social media, but I believe he was a pioneer of this content on TikTok and the like. Made a big name."

"Popular then?" you follow up.

"Undoubtedly."

"I detect a tone in your voice?"

"Ah, you noticed it. I can respect the man's hard work, but he was insufferably arrogant. If you've not solved a puzzle and you listen to him, he'll make out he's a god. If you have solved a puzzle and listen to him, he'll make out he did it three weeks ago and you're too slow to bother with. As I said, most listeners were casuals, overawed by an apparent ability."

Turn to section 113.

You ask, "Do you know anyone who would be angry at this second victim?"

Hewitt leans back into his seat and grins a toothy smile. "What makes you so certain it's a second victim? You don't have any DNA from either crime scene I hear, so what makes you think he's the second? Why not the first in his own world? I am not convinced, neither in this interview or the last one, that you've made a link between the two dead men and The Path. Maybe they both happened to walk it, but if you looked at every murder that had happened in the UK in the last week, wouldn't it be perfectly usual for some of them to have the same hobby? You might as well be out there finding the model trainset killers, or the Man Utd Murderer. Do you see what I mean?"

"I know what you mean."

To ask did you know Gareth Hyax, turn to section 232.
To ask where they were at the time of Hyax's murder, turn to section 102.
To ask if Hewitt has any ideas about the murder, turn to section 5.
To leave Hewitt, return to section 129.

37

"As you regard yourself as the face of the Catan Cartel," you begin to Miss Krasinski, "how about telling me about the other members?"

"In what sense?"

"How do you see them?"

"See them... we're not a very tight-knit bunch, we wouldn't ring each other up for a heart to heart, but we are very competitive with each other. What I'd say is we are fierce opponents for the rest, but we respect each other too. I wouldn't look at the other three and doubt the skills of any of them. Iron sharpens iron and all that. I'm the leader of a good group. I guess I can go a bit further. Greg is just a big softy, you can push his buttons easily, and people who don't know him often do, but I know him. Baxter gets obsessed with games but it's tough to say whether anything comes close to his love of his cat. Maybe The Path has, but he treats her like a queen. Jay's a proofreader, and he isn't afraid to send your Christmas cards back with errors highlighted, but we still like him anyway. You've got to have a thing haven't you, you've got to have a thing."

"What's yours?" you ask.

"Television. I've been told the camera loves me."

To ask more about The Path, turn to section 14.
To ask other questions, return to section 251.

To ask more about The Path, turn to section 14.
To ask other questions, return to section 251.

⬩ 38

"Mr Weald," you begin, "where were you on the night of Mr Webb's death?"

Jay instantly blurts out, "Now that's more like it!"

"Thank you."

"But..." and he seems to see a chance to turn the tables. "Does that ever work?"

"How do you mean?"

Jay explains, "In all your years in the police force, when you've asked, 'where were you', did anyone ever answer, 'at the victim's house stabbing a knife into them.'"

"Generally speaking if they don't have an alibi they say no comment," you answer honestly.

"Ah, and I am supposed to give you an alibi now, that wasn't just a friendly question, this is where I prove I was nothing to do with it."

39

"I suppose, 'Jay', that is exactly the current situation."
"In that case I shan't say no comment, I shall tell you the truth, I was out for a run. I don't know if you can tell my BMI from that distance and with myself in this excellent coat, but I run a mean 5K, and a damned sight more. I do all the park runs round here and one day I might try the London marathon, although I'd have to do some charity thing to be allowed in and that just looks hassle."

Turn to section 285.

˙ 39

You're in an interview room in Sheffield's police headquarters. DC Robertson is to your left, and she's turning on the recording device. Opposite you is the man you arrested at the bowling green, his scraggly beard unkempt and a scratch on his forehead from the tackle. Next to him is a tired looking lawyer.
"Mr... Franks," you begin.
"Yeah."
"How do you know Winnie Forrest?"
"No comment," the suspect replies, as is his right.
"Did Winnie Forrest approach you, as evidenced in this series of emails?" and you hold up the printouts.
"No comment."
"Did you agree to find The Path's final treasure, the Panda, in exchange for a payment of two thousand pounds?"
"No comment."
"Did you then demand Winnie Forrest give you two hundred thousand pounds or you'd tell the police?"
"No comment."

"Why did you come to the bowling green today?"

"No comment."

"Did you come because Winnie emailed you to say she had the money, and you emailed back to say you'd be there?"

"No comment."

"Then how do we interpret these emails?"

"No comment."

"At this time," and you show the suspect a date and time, "a man called Webb was murdered. Do you have an alibi for that murder?"

"No... sorry, what the fuck? A murder?" the suspect reacts with shock.

"Yes, we are investigating two murders connected to The Path."

"Nah man, nah, I ain't into that man, I ain't killing no one. Whatever the fuck else is going on here, I swear I didn't kill anyone."

You are, given the situation and the watertight alibis he now gives, going to believe him.

Return to section 129.

Return to section 129.

↳40

"So it's a puzzle book? Like that one in Ampthill when I was a kid?" Robertson asks you as she drives through Sheffield.

"Exactly. It's a set of puzzles which point to a location, which has something worth a hundred grand, or to put it the official way, an arcane journey through the mysteries of the cosmos to find a fabled object which happens to be worth a hundred grand."

"Oh, fancy stuff then, not like my daily word puzzle."

41

"I've read some of The Path, and it's like your daily word puzzle was smothered in chintz."

"Oh, speaking of things when I was a kid, chintz! Who's it by again?"

"Gato Blanco. Officially. Gato's address isn't freely available, or easily available, and his publishers gave it to me, along with his real name. Reginald Forrest."

"Sorry what?"

"Reginald Forrest."

"I'd have kept the Forrest bit! Right, here we are."

You look out of the car. You weren't sure what you were expecting, but The Path gives the impression the author is a startling mystical and creative mind, not necessarily someone who lives in a new-build house on a cookie cutter 2020s estate. You get out of the car and note the house is almost build flush to the road, with only a two foot front lawn, and ring a doorbell that's still playing a Christmas carol. The door is opened by a man who looks like he should be playing any accountant character in any movie ever. An old brown suit, NHS glasses.

"Hello?"

"Hello there, are you Reginald Forrest, aka Gato Blanc?" The author instantly looked nervous, "I really hope you're about to show me a police badge..."

"Yes, here I am, Inspector, and this is DC Robertson."

"Oh thank God."

"You seem nervous?" you ask.

"I am, I am! This book has turned out to be a nightmare. Why don't you come in, have some coffee, and we can talk."

A few minutes later you have a drink in a mug that's advertising a videogame, and a plate of biscuits are put down. Reginald comes and sits down in a living room that's almost entirely free of decoration. He sees you looking. "My wife is very minimalist; my stuff is kept to my office. Speaking of my wife..."

"Hello," says the woman who's just unlocked the front door and come in. She's well-dressed, short and stocky and holding a handful of unopened letters which, you notice, weren't posted through any letter box. "Are you the police?"

"Yes, yes we are."

"Oh thank goodness, I'm Winnie, you've finally come about the harassment."

You turn and look at Robertson, then back to the Forrests. "Firstly, do you prefer me to call you Reginald or Gato?"

"Reginald, please."

"Secondly, we aren't purely here about the harassment, by which I believe you mean a series of threatening letters you have received."

"Oh?"

"I am sad to say I am investigating the murder of a blogger who was obsessed by your book."

"... nuts."

"To that end, what can you tell me about The Path?"

"I thought it would be a great way to make some money and play a great game with people. Turns out, it's been more trouble than it's worth... and if there's been a murder..."

"You would say the author, Gato Blanc, is more of a character for you, and the book entirely made up?"

"Oh yes, it's a pure puzzle from my head, not from my world."

Turn to section 17.

41

For this round of interviews, you have asked to meet the members of the Catan Cartel individually at their homes. They have all agreed.

For Baxter Hewitt you may add five minutes and turn to section 115.
For Greg Helsh you may add five minutes and turn to section 20.
For Caroline Krasinski you may add five minutes and turn to section 198.
For Jay Weald you may add five minutes and turn to section 253.
Otherwise return to section 46.

42

"Did you know a man called Harold Webb?" you ask.
Hewitt instantly replies, "No."
"He was a gamer and puzzle solver from…"
"I know who he was, I'm not an idiot."
"You just said…"
"Know implies some sort of familiarity or relationship," Hewitt explains patronisingly, "but I do my work and I knew he was out there and working on the puzzle."
"Okay, so you've met him?"
"You know I have, that's why we're here. He came to the group once. Complete waste of time for me."
"How so?"
"Webb was a blogger. He posted everything he did online to gain as large a social media following as possible. I suppose he was trying to make puzzle solving a full-time job, so it's easy for someone like me to drop into his blog

twice a week, see what's he's done, and attend a meeting where he shows up. That does not," and he raps the table for each word, "mean I knew him. I knew him less than my cat."

"Does your cat solve puzzles?"

"My cat is a pedigree and is very clever, but alas her skills lie in hunting and killing small things."

Turn to section 219.

◆ 43

You return with Robertson to the police headquarters and swing by the digital forensics' lab. When you enter, you're impressed to find a man wearing a full, pristine white lab coat, with a pocket containing small screwdrivers sticking up, not pens.

"Hello," you begin, but the expert sees the laptop in your hands and comes right over.

"What have we got here?" he asks.

"We suspect this was stolen from a murder victim, and the killer tried to have it broken into. Anything you can sort out for us?"

"So let me take this, stick a power cable in," and he picks one off a wall unit, "and then we'll have a look." The machine powers up, and a starting screen is displayed.

"Oh yeah, no problem, there's no encryption on this, it's just a normal Windows password. I'll get it cracked for you," and he turns the machine off and starts to plug other cables in. You're not sure whether to come back later, or offer to go get the man a coffee, and by the time you've decided on the latter and opened your mouth the expert turns and says, "Here we go, completely open for you. Want me to copy it?"

"That was quick."

"Security is just in your head. The owner's head. You know what I mean."

Turn to section 181 to examine the laptop.

⁕ 44

"I suppose you're gonna say it," Krasinski says to you.

"Sorry?"

"Go on, you want to do it."

"You'll have to clarify?"

"Like they do on the telly, go on ask, ask me 'where were you the night of the murder?'"

"Yes, sometimes being a detective is like repeating lines from the box. Okay, where were you the night of the murder?"

"I was at home watching television all night. Might have heard someone say that line!"

"All night?"

"Yes, I was at school at my usual time, then had a meeting, so got home at 4:30 in the afternoon, settled in to do some prep, cooked dinner from 6:00 until 7:00, then watched the television to unwind. I know I'm not supposed to say this, they may only be little children, but they can be incredibly difficult little people to deal with. To be honest, they're as rude as Webb was sometimes."

"I see," you reply, taking no side.

"I daresay some of these kids are more unruly than your criminals!" You doubt it, but you don't reply, which leads her to say, "Is that offensive? Ah well. I suppose you deal with murderers; I suppose this is about a murderer. You're used to rougher people than me."

46

Turn to section 29.

● **45**

"Given your views on The Path, what do you hope to get out of it?"

"Oh, I suppose you expect me to say something like, 'if I deconstruct the path' I'll be able to better it with my own work, but let's be honest, I would be misleading you and the police don't traditionally like that. No, I just want the money and the fame, who wouldn't? If I did solve the Path, I'd be all over the television, and I could use the money to stop proofreading, work full-time on the Murder Wall, and ride the publicity to launch and sell it. Not that I've thought about it much at all, as you can see... It's not ending world hunger, but it is my dream. Of course to complete the Path I'd have to devote time given to Murder Wall, but then I wouldn't have finished Murder Wall to sell when I did the Path... such a balancing of issues that Gato never envisioned, I'm sure."

"Probably not," you reply, and Jay has a little chuckle at it all.

To ask Jay about the other members of the group, turn to section 265.

Otherwise, turn back to section 280.

● **46**

Gain the Keyword GREEN.

If you've been to this section before, please skip to the options and select one. Otherwise, read on.

It's a new day, and you are back at your makeshift desk with a strong cup of coffee and a good breakfast inside you. Robertson has arrived, and she's eating croissants with enough butter to put off a leading chef. You have a number of options open to you.

If you have not spoken to members of the Catan Cartel, you can do so now by adding five minutes and turning to section 212.
If you have already spoken to them once, you may do your second set of interviews; turn to section 41.
Otherwise, you may now conduct a third set of interviews, go to section 218.

New options:
⟩ You can follow up a recent call from Baxter, add five minutes and turn to section 279.
• To look at a man who has come in and confessed, add five minutes and turn to section 13.

Old but still valid lines of enquiry if you haven't followed them up before:
To speak to the author of The Path, who's reported threatening letters, add five minutes and turn to section 40.
To investigate another report of clothing being burned at night, add five minutes and turn to section 199.
To follow up a suspicious report from an angry farmer, add five minutes and turn to section 282.
If you have the keyword LETTERS, you may add five minutes and turn to section 120.
If you have the keyword MAIL, you may add five minutes and turn to section 154.
If you have the keyword NIGHT, you may add five minutes and turn to section 191.

If you have the keyword LAPTOP, you may add five minutes and turn to section 85.

To hold a press conference for public aid, add five minutes and turn to section 69.

To follow up a call from your technicians about a laptop, add five minutes and turn to section 114.

To follow up a letter claiming to be 'from the killer', add five minutes and turn to section 3.

To follow up a report about odd traffic, add five minutes and turn to section 33.

If you have the keyword SNEAK, you may turn to section 28.

47

"I assume you've seen the coverage of Mr Webb's murder and the discovery of his body?" you ask Hewitt.
"Yes, yes, I have. It made the morning television, although I haven't got to a newspaper yet."
"As such, what are your views on the killing? Any ideas or insights I might find helpful?"
Hewitt stifles a laugh, then grins, "Actually I do have some thoughts on it all. I think you're completely barking up the wrong tree, to use an ancient phrase."
"How so?"
"You're in the wrong place. Totally the wrong place. The killer is surely in the same locality as the victim, it will all be happening back 'on your patch' as I'm sure you say. There's nothing to suggest the killer's anything to do with Sheffield. In fact we should all be complaining you've got Gato and us on your list of people to question at all. Will you be going to the gaming groups in Glasgow for information? No, no I did not think you would."
"You seem very certain."

"We're mostly killed by people we know, correct?"
"Yes."
"Well there we go. You're on a fool's errand and your colleagues back home will be solving it."
"Mostly."

Turn to section 108.

48

"Do you have any ideas on the case?" you ask Caroline.
"Yes, I think you're completely on the right track with your theory that it's a traveller."
"That's my theory?"
"Yes, and let's face it, what other option is there? But I'm not stupid Inspector, I know the conclusion to make about that."
"Which is?"
"I must keep my progress completely hidden. Of course I do that anyway for fear someone gets ahead of me, but what I'm specifically saying is I can't give any hint I'm doing well, and God forgive I actually say I'm nearly done, because if I do someone will come and murder me too! I don't want to be the third victim, so I've cut right back on my socials, my writing, everything. No one is hearing a word about The Path out of me besides oh how hard it is, I've no chance. Would you say that was a good idea Inspector?"
"It does seem a sensible course of action. No one wants to paint targets at this point."

To ask did you know Gareth Hyax, turn to section 248.
To ask where they were at the time of Hyax's murder, turn to section 65.

To ask if they know anyone angry at Hyax, turn to 208.
To leave Caroline, return to section 129.

❧ 49

"What happened at the group, and what happened to make you regret meeting him?" you ask Greg.

"Arrogant," he replies. "A really arrogant man, who thought he was better than us. Snooty. Yeah, snooty. Looking down his nose at us, all that. He only came to see if we'd tell him the answer, and I reckon that's the last time I organise a speaker or a guest or whatever. I judged him wrong. Not the best judge me, people are harder than puzzles cos people don't follow logic or rules."

"I know this sounds a daft question given what you just said," but you need to ask it anyway, "but did you have any contact with Webb after the meeting?"

"Nah, I put him on ignore. Everything on ignore. I would not allow him back to the group."

"He wanted to come?"

"I dunno, I blocked him."

"Quite."

"I reckon he wouldn't though, not with…"

"With what?" you ask.

"With… what… happened…"

"And what did happen."

"You know, yeah, you know, you're trying to trap me."

"I assure you Greg, I really don't know. What happened that meant he wouldn't likely come back."

"Yeah, so," and he looks at the floor, "you're gonna judge me for this, you're gonna take it all wrong."

"Please tell us, Greg."

"The guy was getting rude and disrespectful of me, and I stood up and shouted at him, and I'm a big guy, I got big lungs, and I got a bit angry, and I shouted at him."

Turn to section 228.

50

While you're waiting for the firefighters to do their stuff, you notice a woman standing by a car watching too. She's glued to the scene with a face set between horror and worry, and you introduce yourself and discover she was the receptionist of Phyllis Wright. You take the chance to ask some questions.

"Do you have any idea why Mrs Wright called me today?"

"None. I was late in, I had a headache and said I'd get in when I could and do the paperwork... do you think that saved my life?"

"Perhaps. Could a client have said something to Mrs Wright?"

"We have all sorts, but I don't know of anything that would have... well I do know all our clients, and I am sort of sworn to secrecy, but I honestly don't know anything."

"She said it was about the puzzle book The Path. Has anyone in the office ever mentioned The Path?"

"Inspector, what can I legally tell you?"

"Whatever you have to."

"I know three of the clients who've been coming in recently have spoken to me, and seemingly everyone, about The Path."

"Can you tell me their names?"

"Okay. I can. Mr Hewitt, Mr Weald and Mr Helsh have all spoken to Mrs Wright."

"Thank you."

To speak to Phyllis' husband, turn to section 7.
To wait and speak to the scene of crime team about their findings, turn to section 222.
To move on in the investigation, turn to section 46.

51

It's half-an-hour later, and you're leaning over the screen of a laptop. It's not yours but belongs to a young woman you've only just met, but who knows Toby Olney a whole lot more. You observe the timestamp as it moves through the period you know Webb was murdered, and it proves Olney's story: you see him arrive, come out to meet a pizza delivery, go back in, and leave much later with renewed swagger. His alibi checks out.

You thank the woman and reassure her no one else needs to know about this, then you head back to the station. A short while later and Stewart is annotating the whiteboard to close off this avenue, and DCI Bakshi comes in and calls you over. You find yourself huddling with your superior, who evidently has some advice for you in this case.

"Hello Inspector. I know you've got to pursue all the avenues in these cases, but just a gentle reminder that not everything is relevant, and everything costs time. You might find, later on, that making a mistake like Olney costs you resources better used elsewhere."

He leaves you to resume the investigation.

Turn to section 100.

The Night Before

A car door opens, and a man slips inside. He's holding two recently poured cups of coffee from a nearby filling station, and he passes one to the woman behind the driving seat.

"So what does the constable want us to do again?" the newcomer asks.

"How did you make your grade with the memory of a haddock?" the driver replies.

"I was too busy remembering your obscene drink order."

"This," and a photograph is held up, "is Caroline Krasinski, and we are going to see if she stays home tonight or goes out."

"I see."

"No, you don't."

"No?"

"Because she just walked past. Right, out of the car and follow her, I'll bring the car at distance."

"Shit."

The man gets out of the car. He's casually dressed, jeans and jacket, with a baseball cap for a sport he doesn't understand, and he set out to follow the woman in front of him at a safe distance. He sips on his coffee as they walk the streets, and he's ready to leap on a bus or tram if needed. But after ten minutes of walking, including one very steep hill, the target knocks on a door and goes inside. The man pauses, sips his coffee, and his car pulls up behind him.

After he's got inside, he says, "I guess we wait."

Turn to section 139.

"We understand that Mr Webb arranged a meeting with you, with the Catan Cartel, to discuss The Path. Is that correct?" you ask.

"Yes," Hewitt replies.

"Did you attend that meeting?"

"Yes, but you know that already, or we would not be having this little question and answer session. Perhaps if you were more direct with your questions..."

"Would you like to give me your account of it?" You lean back into the hard, upright wooden chair.

"He contacted us, one of the others. A message went out, do we want to do this. There was a general feeling among the group that it would be a good idea and he was invited. Again, one of the others agreed time and place, but nonetheless we met, had a fruitless conversation and all went home."

"Why did you go?"

"Me? I gather every scrap of information about The Path, because the moment you ignore someone is the moment they bite you, but it became apparent he hadn't got any information we hadn't worked out ourselves. Complete waste of time, and the man was a borderline fraud pretending he knew."

To ask about the others in the group, turn to section 32.
To ask about The Path, turn to section 79.
To ask a different question, turn back to section 231.

"Mr Weald, do you know anyone with any reason to kill Hyax?"

"Yes," Jay says triumphantly.

"Who?"

"The entire subscribers list of Puzzle! magazine."

"I think I see what you're implying..."

"If everyone has been killed because they are close to finding The Path's answer, then everyone who wants to solve The Path must be on the list of suspects."

"Most of the population wouldn't kill to stop that though," you remind him.

"Most, but if you need a reason to narrow down from, that's it. Now I don't know how you'll narrow it down, but I assure you, that's where you're going to find the killer."

"You've gone pale?" you notice.

"I have I suppose, yes. Because let's face it Inspector, if people near the end are at risk, who is also near the end? That's right, me! I might become a victim!"

To ask, 'Did you know Gareth Hyax?' turn to section 259.

To ask where they were at the time of Hyax's murder, turn to section 107.

To ask if Jay has any ideas about the murder, turn to section 144.

To leave Jay, return to section 129.

"Can you follow that man?" you ask, and you see the person disappear off the footage and reappear half-an-hour later, going back the other way. They're dressed in the same manner as the suspected killer of Webb. Did they buy multiples of this non-descript 'uniform'? The camera coverage is sparse, but you see the suspect go down the stairs, round some corners and then... they walk off one camera and don't appear on the next one. As you don't think a ghost is to blame you ask, "Where have they gone?"

"Err..." the manager seems to struggle to recall before concluding, "there's a staff exit door there. He must have gone through it."

"Does it look to you like the person we were following knew the route through the hotel?" you ask.

"Yeah, they knew how to come in and out the staff doors so they won't have come through reception, and if they got into your room, they must have taken a key. We have no cameras in the staff corridors."

"Ex-staff member maybe?" you ask.

"No, could be anyone."

"Why do you say that?"

"Our plans are on the internet?"

"Sorry?"

"We've had some legal issues, and, well, someone published the plans for the hotel on the internet. Wouldn't be hard to find it."

"Then why is it still there?" you ask concerned.

"We just figured it was cheaper not to sue it down."

You nod sadly. "I will be leaving for a new hotel soon."

Turn to section 109.

56

"But now you know that, Miss Krasinski, perhaps you could follow its logic for us. Say I was interested in people in the Catan Cartel. Do you think anyone in your group could have committed this murder, or be involved in some way?"

Krasinski nods to herself, and it's evidently the first time she's considered the concept. "I would say... no. We are all good people, and none of us would ever commit a murder, and if we did, we'd have a good reason like they'd killed our parents or something. Like Batman."

Robertson starts to say, "That's not..." and stops.

"You never know what people are thinking," you add.

"I guess my answer's no help for you is it. But I'm going to be honest, I don't want to land anyone in it, and I don't think any of us would do it. I think you have this whole thing wrong." She crosses her arms forcefully. Maybe look closer to home, we're all a bit weird in our ways, aren't we," and she finishes by looking at you.

Return to section 251 to continue your questioning.

57

You move down the right-hand path and follow the single set of prints. They're clear, and you're able to walk for a good minute following them before you come to a small clearing, on which the path splits into two again. You ponder which route to take before your vision explodes in stars and everything goes black.

The next thing you know, you're aware of a heavy pain in the back of your head, as if something is repeatedly hitting you... before you realise that's your heartbeat, and with every pulse your brain hurts. When you're able to open your heavy eyelids, you find yourself in a white room, in a metal bed, in different pyjamas to those you've ever worn.

"Oh thank God you're awake," a voice you recognise says, and it takes you a moment to realise it's Robertson, and she's sat by your bedside.

"What? Where?" you ask.

"We found you in the wood, you'd been unconscious a while, someone smashed you on the head."

"Wood... the woman... the killers..."

"Don't you worry, you're going to be in bed recovering for a while, the investigation has been reassigned.

For you, Inspector, this is the end of the story, unless you return to section 261 and pick a different path.

58

You look around the small clearing, focusing on the three tracks which lead off. While Stewart's boots seemed to have repelled the mud, all the tracks have footprints left in it. Sometimes, the rain can be a help.

The path you came up has clear signs of multiple feet going back and forth along it, including your own, a chaos forensics will have to sort out, but the other paths are much clearer.

The path to the left has multiple sets of footprints, but all are leading into the clearing. You believe the jogger came this way, but other people have too. Meanwhile, the right-hand path has just one set of partial prints leading away from the clearing, and the shallow, half prints suggest running.

The outward bound training you received as a child is telling you to look at breakages to plants and tree branches, but these don't reveal anything clear, they could have been made yesterday.

"Do you know which way to go Inspector?" Stewart asks.

"Yes," you reply.

Head down the left path, turn to section 160.
Head down the right path, turn to section 236.
Head down the path you came in on, turn to section 105.

59

"Can anyone corroborate that you were out running?"
"Corroborate…"
"Give you an alibi, say if you were running with someone…"
"I know what corroborate means, I'm just trying to think. I don't run with people, that would be a bore, I… oh yes!" He leaps out of his seat, "I track all my runs on the app on my phone! It will show you exactly where I was!" He stabs at his phone with a thin finger, and then thrusts it towards you.
It takes you a moment to understand what you're looking at, and you hold the phone so you and Robertson can look at it. You navigate a few menus and can only come to one conclusion.
"There's no runs listed for the night in question," you tell Jay.
"What? No, let me look again…" He urgently smashes a series of on screen buttons, then sinks back into his chair. "I can't have had the app on. I'm always doing it. I swear I've lost all my record of my best time too over recent weeks. So the app's a loss then?"
"Yes."
"Then… I don't have any 'corroboration' to give you I'm afraid."
You nod and make a note.

Return to section 280 to pursue other questions.

60

With Robertson busy on other aspects of the case, you leap in a car and drive round to the address you were given. The satellite navigation on the dashboard does the trick, and you admit to yourself it's nice to be driving rather than have Robertson chauffeur you around... even if you don't recognise the streets you're driving though and have to be guided by a computer's voice. However you soon arrive at the place. There's a small parade of shops, including a restaurant, a hairdressers, and a corner store, and above it is a series of offices. There's a very neat, smart sign listing the office tenants, so you park up in the bays in front and go over.
It does indeed list the office of Phyllis Wright.
You push open the door and step inside the bottom of a stairwell, complete with nice plant. Up the stairs you go, and you turn right, to find the heavy fire door with the sign of Mrs Wright's business, and a button to summon the receptionist.
You press and wait.
Nothing happens.
After a while you press the bell again, but no one answers, so you decide to give the door a push.

Turn to section 193.

61

"Anything else?" Krasinski asks.

"Yes, just following that up, can anyone corroborate what you just said?"

"About staying at home?"

"Yes, can anyone give you an alibi?"

"Oh. No. I was just relaxing on my lonesome. I don't suppose a half drunk bottle of wine and the history of my cable provider is much of a help is it."

"I'm afraid not."

"In that case... oh dear I don't think there is any way I can prove that to you. Does this count against me? Does this make me a suspect? Oh, I'm going to be a suspect."

"No it doesn't," you explain, "but as you say, it's a question we have to ask and it's helpful in establishing what's going on."

"Hmm. I hope you don't think I'm being lazy just sitting in on my own, I had to fill my head with puzzle answers so what better than to consume the soaps, because they get asked about, then some documentaries, bit of reading, all the information I fill my head with. And, of course, the time I spend researching The Path."

"But you didn't do anything with The Path that night?"

"No, I didn't."

You have gained the Keyword NIGHT. Make a note of it. Then turn to section 153 to ask more questions.

₁ 62

With the body already being examined, you allow yourself to be guided through to the hotel, where you head up to the room Hyax was staying in. You find a uniformed officer on the door keeping it secure, but you are of course allowed inside.

It's a small room, one of the hotel's cheapest. You don't know the puzzle magazine industry, but you suspect it doesn't allow for much ostentatious hospitality. There's a table with a television on, and a news channel is playing. There's a half-empty cup of coffee next to it, clothes in a pile on a chair, and on the bed printouts of a text document are spread in an arc where someone would have been sitting.

"Yunno," Robertson begins, "I get the feeling Mr Hyax didn't mean to be out for long, or to be going out at all."

"I agree. Someone... interrupted him and lured him?"

"I'd say so."

You lean over and look at the text that was being edited. It's a long article about The Path.

"Certainly seems like it could be connected to Webb..." you say. The one thing you never want in a murder case is the realisation there might be many more murders.

"Hello?" the uniformed officer by the door calls.

"Yes?"

"I think it's definitely connected," she tells you.

"Okay, what have you found?"

"Puzzle! magazine," the officer begins, "you can find it in WHSmith's, and newsagents and all that, my gran buys it. So I went to their website while I was guarding, and you'll never guess what...?"

"Go on..."

"Editor Hyax posted this morning that he was mere days away from solving The Path. He'll announce it in a future follow up issue."

"Then we have a repeat killer," you say sadly.

You have several immediate options:

° To examine Hyax's phone, turn to section 179.

° To search the CCTV cameras in the area, turn to section 143.

PTO

63

To follow up the examination of the body, turn to section 31.

When you are finished with these lines of enquiry, return to your hotel for the night by turning to section 124.

63

"Have you had any further thoughts on the murders?" you ask Hewitt.

"My thoughts have stayed the same and you haven't changed them. You think Mrs Wright was killed by the Path killer... but why? What reason have you got? It could just as easily be someone else and now your serial killer has magically grown to three victims while two or three killers are walking free."

"The M.O. is the same," you explain.

"M.O... modus operandi? You're claiming they were stabbed by a common household object and that's so unusual they're all connected. Poppycock. At the very least find who killed Mrs Wright and sort that out. Least you could do. Shame I can't bet on Caroline solving all this before you do. Maybe someone from the Sheffield constabulary should take over."

To ask if he knew Phyllis Wright, turn to section 213.
To ask what they were doing at the time of the murder / arson, turn to section 255.
To ask if they knew any connection between Phyllis and The Path, turn to section 125.
To move on, return to section 218.

"Did you know a man called Harold Webb?" you ask. Hewitt instantly replies, "No."

"He was a gamer and puzzle solver from…"

"I'm aware of who he was."

"You just said…"

"I didn't know him," Hewitt explains patronisingly, "to me that implies some sort of familiarity or relationship. But I knew he was out there and working on the puzzle."

"Okay, so you've met him?"

"You know I have, that's why we're here. He came to the group once. But my interaction was mainly online."

"How so?"

"Hewitt was a blogger. He posted everything he did online to gain as large a social media following as possible. I suppose he was trying to make puzzle solving a full-time job, so it's easy for someone like me to drop into his blog twice a week, see what's he's done, and attend a meeting where he shows up. That does not," and he raps the table for each word, "mean I knew him. I knew him less than my cat."

"Does your cat solve puzzles?"

"My cat is a pedigree and is very clever, but alas her skills lie in hunting and killing small things."

Turn to section 157.

65

If you have the keyword SNOOKER, turn to section 173.

"Caroline," you begin, "where were you the night of Mr Hyax's murder?"

"I regret to tell you, I was asleep here in my lounge, in front of the television. I've been sleeping off hours with my stress at the murder, and I had nodded off when I should have been studying. I realise such lax behaviour isn't going to make you think me any less innocent seeing as I have no alibi but... I can assure you I am not a killer, much less a serial killer, and I don't know what else I can say to put your mind at rest. Perhaps... I should start logging myself in and out somehow so you can focus elsewhere. Am I a suspect, Detective? In all honesty, do you consider me one?"

"Yes, Miss Krasinski," you admit, "you are."

"Are all the Catan Cartel?"

"At this point, yes, you all are." You watch as she nods sadly.

To ask, 'Did you know Gareth Hyax? turn to section 248.
To ask if they know anyone angry at Hyax, turn to section 208.
To ask if Caroline has any ideas about the murder, turn to section 48.
To leave Caroline, return to section 129.

● 66

"Where were you on the night of the murder?" you ask with a totally straight face, not expecting Hewitt to start openly laughing. "A private joke?"

"No, no," Hewitt replies, "but I've been waiting for you to say that; it's the most police question ever isn't it, where were you."

You tilt your head and say, "It was pretty magical to say it for the first time, yes."

"I bet."

"So, where were you?"

"Easy, same place I am every evening, in my pharmacy. I don't have a partner unless you count my gorgeous cat, I don't have kids, but what I do have is a thriving business I pay closer attention to. Every night I restock, stock take, do accounts, prepare prescriptions, so I don't know how much you know about chemists or shopkeeping in general, but I sit and sort it all out."

You nod, "And is there anything which can corroborate that? Are there other staff members with you?"

"If there were they would demand payment. No, there were no humans there with me, but luckily everything is fully covered by closed-circuit television. I can ring," and he pulls out a mobile phone, "and get the footage secured for you?"

Turn to section 87.

67

Mrs Helsh spends a while thinking, then agrees, she will file a complaint with the police. Robertson collects her car, then collects you and Anna, as you find out she's called, and takes you to the station. The domestic violence unit swings into action, and later on that day Greg is arrested on multiple counts. Later on, he will be charged and appear in court, and after that, found guilty.

Greg will not be out of custody for the remainder of your investigation. You have done a great service in bringing this case to the police and getting justice for Anna. Additionally, thanks to her testimony, Greg is no longer a suspect in your murder case.

Acquire the Keyword ORANGE.

Return to section 46.

"What do you do for a living?" you ask Greg.
"This is another dig at me, innit?" Greg snaps, voice rising, "You know I'm self-employed cos I got fired, cos I'm really unemployed, but you listen to me, I'm trying to make the best of it. Lost my job but now I'm a full-time app designer, coder and reviewer."
"Full-time reviewer?"
"YouTube channel; rips these useless twats to shreds. 'Everything Wrong With This App' it's called, and I give stuff a right bollocking."
"I see."
"And you lot, you work for the cops, but I got my own company, G-Man Games, I'm G-Man cos I'm, Greg yeah…"
"Yes."
"And we do some games, some other useful apps. I'm useful, even if one little incident has got in the fucking way. But best thing that ever happened to me, going alone."
"I respect your hard work," you tell him honestly. A little flattering seems to calm him.
"Do any of these apps relate to The Path?"
"Nah, that's a hobby for me, I love my puzzles but it's pure escapism from the stresses of real life, yeah."
"I imagine reviews and things online can be tough, you'd have to have a thick skin?"

"Lots of rude fuckers online, lots of rude fuckers, but I tell 'em, you got something to say, we'll meet up and we'll see if you say it."

Turn to section 276.

Turn to section 276.

69

You stand as a microphone is pinned to your jacket, and the woman doing it asks, "Have you ever done a press conference before?"
It's all you can do not to roll your eyes, but you politely reply, "I've done many over the years..."
"Well you haven't done any here. Now this mic, it's gonna make everything you say loud, so don't call anyone a bastard under your breath."
"You say that like it's happened?"
"Do you think I'd be bothering lecturing an adult like they're a child if that hadn't actually happened?"
"Fair point," you concede.
"You will give a presentation on the current facts, and then you will take questions from the audience. It's a big room but there's a lot of journalists, so expect them to range from the actually giving a damn to people who just want to slag you off in print."
"Pretty standard then," you sigh.
"Unlike all those government press conferences, we expect our speakers to have their own buttons to change the slides," and she forces a small plastic clicker into your hand. "This is it. Don't click unless you're ready. Now I've checked your slides to prevent another Italian incident."
"I assume that refers to something that shouldn't have been on the slides..."
"Bingo. Right, go take your seat and we'll get started."

Turn to section 106.

⚜ 70

You and DC Robertson leave the hotel and head to her car, a deep-blue Mini. She's only driving it for a short while before you leave the commercial heart of the city and find yourself in a decaying industrial part. That's when you spot a uniformed officer standing by an entrance gate holding an umbrella. When you've parked up, said hello and walked in, you can see the immediate target: in this yard, surrounded by sad old brickwork and weeds, is a large old barrel... and someone's recently set a fire in it.

"We have a report last night," Robertson explains, "of a blaze in this yard. The Fire Brigade attended, and they called us as, well, let me put it this way: someone burned a pile of clothing in that barrel last night. We can't get much information from it, I mean DNA, and hair, and stuff is surely gone but here's what we worked out: you can walk here, all the way from the station, without being seen on CCTV, and they could have changed, burnt this, and headed off, again with no CCTV."

"Thanks," you reply, and look around.

"And I know what you're thinking," Robertson adds, "but not everything got burned. There was a shoulder bag down by the side of the barrel. SOCO have been here, they've got it and there's no laptop in it but..." she holds her phone up and shows you a photo of the bag. It's the same type the figure in the CCTV was carrying. It really does look like the supposed killer dumped the clothes here and continued on.

You smile, "Which suggests they really are here in Sheffield somewhere still."

Turn to section 75.

71

"…how would you sum Glen up?" you ask Jay.
"He's just a big guy who wears his heart on his… actually Glen's got a violent streak. I don't want to bad-mouth the guy, and I know saying he threw out a guy who later got murdered doesn't paint him in a good light, but in for a penny: I would hate to live with Greg. It would be murder. He'd have me terrified he was going to go off. He seems to like all of the Cartel and put up with us, but I know the rest of the world isn't so lucky. It's his kids I feel for, although… I've never been interested in kids myself. I… wish to stop this line of questioning there."
"How about Caroline and Baxter?"
"Baxter's harmless, in fact that princess of a cat of his is probably more deadly with her birds, and mice, and whatever else cats get up to. As for Caroline, aren't most killers men? Be a good alibi wouldn't it, a female serial killer no one suspects because of millennia of accumulated misogyny."
"Good idea for a puzzle…" you tell Jay. "You can have that one for free." He doesn't laugh, in fact he stands up and says, 'Questioning is over' and walks back over to the Cartel. He won't be saying anything further at the moment.

Turn back to section 212.

If you have the keyword ORANGE, turn to section 189 immediately.

You return to Greg's house, and when he opens the door, your nose is filled with the smell of bacon. Greg sees it's happened and says, "Oh, you know it Inspector, you know it, a good fry up. Nothing beats a hangover like bacon, eggs, sausage, more eggs, hash browns, toast, beans, I could go on..."
"Is there literally anything left to say?" you wonder out loud.
"Well black pudding, tomatoes, mushrooms, all are options, but I don't have those in my fridge today, so yeah. I guess you can't eat on duty, or I'd offer you both a plate. Instead I'll get you some tea. So, what did you want to talk about?"

To ask if he knew Phyllis Wright, turn to section 246.
To ask what they were doing at the time of the murder / arson, turn to section 24.
To ask if they knew any connection between Phyllis and The Path, turn to section 97.
To ask if they have any further ideas on the case, turn to section 273.
Or return to section 218.

ᵥ 73

You take a sip of the coffee the pub have provided you with, note it's surprisingly good, and look at your notes. Then you look at Miss Krasinski and ask, "Have you won many kitchen knives?"

Krasinski's face contorts in confusion, and you can see Robertson to the side of you looking askance too.
"What, err, what has that got to do with anything?" Krasinski asks.
Robertson feels the need to dive in and help you and takes over: "The murder weapon was a kitchen knife, just a common-or-garden kitchen knife. Now I don't know much about quiz shows but I'm sure there's always a set of knives up for grabs."
Krasinski doesn't look reassured. "I've won lots of things that could kill people, from knives to an actual samurai sword, but winning a blade isn't illegal. A kitchen knife. Anyone in the Cartel could just go and buy a set right now and no one would bat an eyelid. That seems a... very odd thing to be asking me."
You nod as you take notes, then say, "Thanks Constable, that was my thinking." Robertson gives you a look that says probably rethink it.

Turn to section 251 to resume questioning.

74

You rush round to find Jay Weald laying on the sofa drinking. He starts to come peacefully as you arrest him, but then he overhears an officer say they can't find Forrest. This starts Jay off and he screams at you, "You should have protected him, you should have protected him."

It is only later that day, when Reginald Forrest's mutilated body is discovered, that it's confirmed you arrested the wrong person. You are taken off the case, and Sheffield's own police take charge, review the material you have collected, and arrest the right killer. You have failed Inspector.

To choose a different suspect return to section 242 or play through the book again and search for more clues.

ᴉ 75

If you have the keyword BLUE, return to section 129.
If you have the keyword GREEN, return to section 46.
If you've been to this section before, please skip to the options and select one. Otherwise, read on.

It's time to set up your new working home. Robertson drives you to a large and smartly designed building and shows you where the most essential piece of equipment is, a coffee machine. You're immediately impressed as it makes a great cup, or a cracking brew, and you note down the model name in case you can persuade your own DCI to pay out for one. Then you're standing in a corner of the major crimes unit's office, where they've kindly cleared you a desk. It's a wide, open room, recently refurbished, with computers utilising the latest software. You have to shake off the odd feeling of setting your laptop down on a desk when you're searching, in part, for a laptop stolen off a desk. Then you exchange introductions with the other detectives, as you'll all be passing each other every day. However, without Stewart, it's down to you to write the shortlist of leads on the whiteboard.
Or is it?
"Hello," Robertson says as she appears behind you and drops her bag next to your desk. "You've got me full-time while we crack this thing, assume you want me to of course?"

"Yes please, the help is appreciated."
"So, what are we going to do next?"

- To speak to the Catan Cartel members, add five minutes and turn to section 212.
- To speak to the author of The Path, who's reported threatening letters, add five minutes and turn to section 40.
- To investigate another report of clothing being burned at night, add five minutes and turn to section 199.
- To follow-up a suspicious report from an angry farmer, add five minutes and turn to section 282.
- If you have the keyword LETTERS, you may add five minutes and turn to section 120.
- If you have the keyword MAIL, you may add five minutes and turn to section 154.
- If you have the keyword NIGHT, you may add five minutes and turn to section 191.
- If you have the keyword LAPTOP, you may add five minutes and turn to section 85.

⁌ 76

When you knock on the door this time, both Forrests stand there having opened it.

"Hello there, us again," and you smile. "Just a few follow-up questions, if we can. Constable Robertson here, if you can go over those details of The Path with Mr Forrest and if I may Mrs Forrest, a few questions in the kitchen about the letters."

Robertson heads off on her diversion mission, and you follow Mrs Forrest into the kitchen.

"You've had them examined already?" she asks excitedly.

"That was a little misdirection, I don't mean threats. I'm going to come right out with this," you begin, "because it might be nothing or it might be everything, but how much does your husband know about the large debts you're in? Or are you hiding everything from him?"

She's turned white and grips a worktop. "How much do you know?"

"I'm allowed to see your financials. I know the numbers, but not the human side."

"I... he's not great with the real world, he lives in his head, my husband, and I love him, and he spent years creating this book and it's world, and he was so happy it was published... and so was I because I thought it would pay our debts off. If anything, we're worse. I would appreciate you not telling him unless... well I can't see how that would be connected to the murder, but in turn, I can see how us sat here lying to you isn't exactly innocent."

"I appreciate your honesty, and it helps me keep a clear picture. Thank you."

Add keyword ALPHA.

Turn to section 75 to return to headquarters.

77

"I have to be honest," Robertson begins as she looks at the screens in front of her, "I'm not sure on the legality of this?"

The member of the digital forensics department who's sat controlling the screens turns and says, "Bosses may monitor workplace emails if they have good reason, follow data protection and have a good reason. One of

CID leaking information to the press fits in with this. So, I've had a search going to look up keywords on all the relevant emails and..."

"What have you found?" you ask.

"First, we looked at everyone they've been emailing, addresses. Then we used keywords like 'editing', 'proofreading', 'on bed', we didn't use Path because that flags up the whole investigation."

"Yes, and what did you find?"

"Nothing."

"Hmm. Nothing?"

"Using search functions on the database, I can't find any emails that show a discussion of the editing, I can't find any suspicious email addresses used, I can't find any evidence of our system being used. Which was a longshot, because it's easy for any detective to use their private phones to leak."

"Fair point, thanks for the time."

To leave this line of enquiry behind, return to section 129.
To give everyone working with you different briefing notes and see what happens, add five minutes and turn to section 237.

To interview everyone working with you, add ten and turn to section 215.

78

You walk down the stairs and out into reception, where the current shift is sat watching their phone which is propped up beneath the top of the desk.

"Excuse me," you begin.

"Hello, how may I help you?" they ask hurriedly removing an ear pod.

"I think someone's been in my room."

"No, I don't... really? What makes you so sure?"

"I don't believe this hotel sends cleaners, and room service, and the like into a room currently occupied, that's right?"

"Yes, that's correct. Our prices are good, but we don't go in during a tenancy."

"Then no one working here had any reason to go into my room."

"Well... I suppose that is correct."

"My things have moved, someone's been in. Has anyone suspicious been seen? Anyone acting oddly, someone who came and left swiftly?"

"Err, you'd have to talk to the other shifts really, but nothing's been logged as unusual. We have a lot of visitors come and go quickly, if you know what I mean, someone acting shiftily isn't unusual at all. We're a city-centre hotel."

"I had better get the cameras checked..." you say out loud.

"Wouldn't bother, they're rubbish. Many of our customers don't want to be filmed."

"Okay, in that case can you book me another hotel please. I'll be leaving now."

"Sure."

Turn to section 109.

79

"What can you tell me about The Path?" you ask Hewitt. He answers, "I assume you don't want a complete page-by-page breakdown of the solution so far discovered, because I will protest to a lawyer about sharing that confidential information."

You smile politely back at him. "No, just in general."

"These puzzle books come out every so often, none of them ever became as popular as Masquerade, which I think you'll find is the masterpiece."

"Not The Path?"

"The Path resonated with a lot of people, I believe, but it's not a great puzzle, not really deserving of the sales, but certainly a hundred thousand pound prize will focus people's attention. As you no doubt know the author is local, and perhaps the solution is too... the Cartel members seized on it quickly. We're trendsetters. We led the way. A lot of almost as dedicated people are following in our footsteps."

"It matters then, that the author is local?"

"Gato Blanc being in the same city... yes, I think it does, perhaps that makes it more personal for us all. Perhaps that's what got us all started. I mean I know Gato's got a real name too, of course, don't put me down as ignorant.

Turn to section 2.

◊ 80

The door is old, peeling paint revealing grey wood, and it's opened by a short man who winces at the daylight. Behind him, you can see the curtains are all closed.

"Police?" he asks keenly.

"Yes, I'm the Inspector and this is Detective Constable Robinson. Are you Abraham Dealve?"

"That I am. I half thought you'd not taken me seriously."

"We take everything seriously, especially confessions."

"Good," he says. "Come in."

He leads you into a living room lit by a single dull bulb, stinking of cigarette smoke.

"Do you wish to come to the station and have a lawyer present?" you ask.

"I don't need a lawyer."

"Okay, what do you have to say to us?"

Dealve sits down and coughs, then begins. "I killed Harold Webb. I stuck a knife in his guts. Left him in a wood. Then I killed Gareth Hyax, different knife, different guts, same results. Left him in a car park. Then I killed Wright, a psychiatrist. Woods again. Killed them all. Left them to rot."

"And why did you kill these three people?" you ask.

"Three? I didn't say just three."

Turn to section 130.

81

You ask Greg, "How did he react?"

"Oh, he scarpered. Ran right off. Rest of the Cartel weren't happy, I reckon, cos I dunno if they found him any better, but they all agreed he'd been rude. Yeah, he didn't like being shouted at."

"Do you not like rude people?" you ask innocently enough.

"Nah, why would I? Why should I? I got a life, and a mind, and I'm a human, and I don't have to take people talking shit to me or starting trouble. So yeah, if some little shit's gonna come into my group of friends and treat me like a servant or something I'm gonna call that little shit out cos I'm a bit shit and I will not fucking have it!" He has been getting louder and louder and finishes shouting and gesturing.

"But you'd never hurt Mr Webb? You didn't hurt Mr Webb?"

"Just his poxy fucking feelings. I'd not kill him, and I don't want you trying to fit me up neither. It's just a game for fuck's sake, you can't kill someone over a fucking game. It's not like the military or something."

"You've been in the military?"

"Nah, just an example where you can kill someone."

Return to section 177 to continue questioning.

82

You say out loud that you must all now arrest Greg Helsh. Given that Greg is currently in police custody this makes everyone look at you strangely, but Robertson offers to accompany you back to the station to see if Greg is still there. However, when you arrive at the station it's clear Robertson sent a message on ahead, and you are sent to see the medical team about your mental state.

It is only later that day, when Reginald Forrest's mutilated body is discovered, that it's confirmed you tried to arrest the wrong person. You are taken off the case, and Sheffield's own police take charge, review the material you have collected, and arrest the right killer. You have failed Inspector.

To choose a different suspect return to section 242 or play through the book again and search for more clues.

❧ 83

You're impressed. Although it's short notice, the whole five-person group who called themselves GWA have gathered together in a central coffee shop, where they've all brought something and sat around tensely. There's no reason to drag this out, but you size up each of the people you'll be asking questions of. Three men, two women, all of the same age group as Webb, and all wearing gaming-related memorabilia. A Resident Evil hat, a Catan t-shirt that says, 'wood for sheep', something which you're reliably informed is a Space Marine backpack.

"Can you all please tell me the last time you saw Harold Webb?" you ask.

"Oh that's easy," says Catan man, "we had our meet up at the weekend. Have any of you seen him since or was that it?" He looks at his friends.

"No, no, that was it for me," one says.

"Same," say another.

"And how was the weekend meeting?" you ask and see them all sigh.

Space Marine woman takes over. "He went on and on about this book, like he always did. Why, has something happened?"

"I'm afraid to have to tell you that Mr Webb was killed last night. We strongly suspect murder."

"Are we suspects?"

"No," you reassure them, "not at this stage. But do any of you know anyone who might want to harm Mr Webb. People he'd fallen out with?"

"Oh yes."

"Yes?" you ask.

Resident Evil man speaks now. "He's no debts we know of, no vices, but he's obsessed with this puzzle. The Path, thinks it'll make him rich and famous, goes on and on and... he's fallen out big time with a gaming group in

Sheffield. The Catan Cartel. They're kinda like us, a local group, and Webb had been in contact with them but... we dunno what was said but it went wrong, and they all argued. He ranted about them."

"Why Sheffield?" you ask.

"The Cartel are all working on The Path. He thought they knew the author; he thought the item wasn't too far from them. But you'll soon know all about that. He did everything on his laptop. Not a phone guy, a laptop one." Ah. You question them further, but nothing new comes up.

You receive the keyword GAME.

Return to headquarters by turning to section 100.

⸎ 84

"Good day, this is the Royal Mail, how can I help you?"

"Hello, I'm an inspector with the police," you begin. "I'm hoping you can help me with a question..."

"Of course Inspector."

"I assume you have rotas of staff and everything, I need to know firstly is Carter Cook still working for you, and what delivery round was he on today?"

"Let me just check..." and you can hear keys being pressed. "Carter Cook is no longer employed by the Royal Mail. There was... am I allowed to say what there was?"

"Was he terminated after drink driving?"

"Yes, that's on his record."

"Thanks, perfect."

You put the phone down and turn to Robertson. "I have a lead, Carter Cook."

"Yes, he's not too bright," Robertson tells you.

"You know him?"

"No, I googled him while you were on the call. He's another vlogger, has a YouTube channel devoted to The Path. A YouTube channel which already has a copy of the letter that was sent being discussed..."

"So... he posted a letter, didn't wait for us to announce it, and went straight for the traffic..."

"Yep. I'm beginning to doubt he's even the killer. Just a gorehound."

"We better go speak to him."

Turn to section 11.

⬗ 85

You catch up with the digital forensics staff working in Sheffield and ask about Greg Helsh's laptop.

"Ah yes Inspector, we've had time to look at it. Why don't you take a seat," the officer says to you.

You sit and say, "You've found a lot then?"

"Well it's interesting. As I'm sure you know, time stamps on your average files aren't a great source of material for us, not very reliable in court, and laptops are the absolute worst for that, even if you do manage to work out they've been connected to the same ISP through the same physical connection and can pin them in a house. It's a whole bag of trouble, and luckily, we've had none of it."

"How so?"

"Well normally when someone's said they've been using a machine, they've at least made some attempt to show they have. Faked it, even if it's really clumsy. But I can assure you Inspector, there is absolutely zero evidence Greg Helsh used this laptop the entire day the murder happened. There's not even a daft fraud, or an email sent

they're claiming. He might as well have not powered it on all day."
"So not only does his alibi have no evidence, it's actually fake?"
"Yes, yes Inspector."
"Thank you."

Turn back to section 75.

86

"Was Phyllis connected to The Path in any way?"
Jay replies, "I doubt it would have been Path related because Phyllis hated The Path, she didn't have much time for it and tried to stop me obsessing over it."
"I see. Do you know of anyone, or any reason, someone would be angry at Mrs Wright?"
"I find it hard to believe any patient of Phyllis would strike her. She was so wonderful, insightful, she really let you walk out of that office with your head held high. But that's not an answer for you so... I know someone else in the Cartel was seeing her. We tend to keep that sort of thing on the downlow in the group, apart from with Caroline, we all open up to Caroline, but she let slip there was another patient. Yeah, yeah, another Cartel member... "

To ask if he knew Phyllis Wright, turn to section 288.
To ask what they were doing at the time of the murder / arson, turn to section 16.
To ask if they have any further ideas on the case, turn to section 110.
Or return to section 218.

"No thanks," you say turning down Hewitt's offer, "I would prefer it if an officer does it instead. DC Robertson?" you finish speaking loudly, and Robertson comes over from keeping the rest of the Cartel in good order. "Can you please contact..."
"... Hewitt's Chemist."
"... Hewitt's Chemist and get their CCTV please."
"Sure thing."
You watch as Robertson uses her phone to google the details of Hewitt's Chemist, ring them and speak. You turn back to the man himself to ask more questions but notice out of the corner of your eye Robertson has pulled a face. You turn once more, unable to lip read the conversation, fascinated to know what's got such a reaction from such a theoretically simple task. Hewitt has turned too, so you study his face and find it impassive, waiting, no clue as to whether he knows what's being discussed. The phone call seems to get more heated, before Robertson clicks the phone off and comes over waving it around in her hand.
"A problem, Inspector."
"Go on, Constable?" you ask, leaning forward in genuine excitement at what this new wrinkle will be.
"The CCTV at the chemist isn't working."

Turn to section 131.

"No, no," you say wagging your finger at the screen. "We're not falling for that."

"What?" Robertson asks.

"That isn't from the killer. We'd be wasting our time if we looked into that, it would be the Yorkshire Ripper all over again."

Robertson leans down and looks at the letter. "Don't tell me, don't tell me..." and you can see her reading it over and over again. Eventually she sighs and says, "What am I missing?"

"Compare that letter with the ones sent to Forrest."

"Oh... err... oh!"

"Exactly. I'm not saying we shouldn't work out who sent these, because we need to charge them with wasting our time, I'm just saying we shouldn't spend our main resources on it."

"Totally agree Inspector," Robertson says nodding.

"Besides, the Panda's Paw sounds like a rubbish thirties pulp villain that'd be drawn totally racist."

"Well, yes, it would."

To continue the investigation, return to section 129.

◆ 89

"That's a lot of research, The Path must mean a lot to you?"

"Yeah, nah, I gotta be honest, I want it for the money and the fame. I got a lot of bills to pay, don't earn much anymore, and The Path would shift me a shitload of apps. And let's face it, when you know you're good enough to solve it, why wouldn't you try? That Gold Panda's worth a hundred grand, and I'd be on telly more than Kras, so... yeah you bet I want to solve it. Especially at the moment. I gotta be honest, if I did solve it, I might have to split it with Kras, cos yunno, they'd put her all over the telly and

I think the cancelling bastards might have a go at me, so I'd cut her in for like twenty five per cent."

"Why Kras, sorry, Miss Krasinski and not Mr Hewitt and Mr Weald?"

"Cos she's a woman I guess." You can feel Robertson trying to control the expression that so desperately wanted to appear on her face. "I don't think it's bad to talk about money. I'm honest yeah, I want the money, no shame in that. All the others want it, but I bet they never say it."

Turn back to section 177 to continue.

90

Mrs Helsh listens to your summary of the case, then starts shaking her head. "I hate to do this to you Inspector, but Greg didn't do it. That first killing you said, he wasn't nowhere near the place you come from... cos he'd found out where I was hiding and come round to shout at me. I got witnesses, who moved him on. See, Greg's always had a foul temper, but he'd started to get violent, started to hit me and... I know it looks easy on the outside to go, but it starts slowly, builds up, and you kinda get used to it even though you're terrified of it... but I always reckoned Greg would kill me one day and in the end that gave me the strength to hide. So I went to a friend's place... turns out he went round everyone in my address book looking for me. Found me, shouted and screamed, and threw his hands. So he ain't your killer but he's a fucking bully all right."

"You didn't come to the police?" Robertson asks.

"Well, what are you going to do?"

"Mrs Helsh, as a detective constable in the force, I can promise you we can take you to a domestic violence shelter, have you looked after by a dedicated unit, and arrest and charge Greg for what he's done as we have witnesses."

"Really?" Mrs Helsh turns to you, "Really?"

"Yes. We can take him off the streets."

Turn to section 67.

91

You're looking through some paperwork when the phone rings. It's expected, and you greet the lady you've been speaking to at the bus service. "Hello there."

"Hello Inspector, I've had a look at our database for you and am pleased to confirm that the driver you were asking about was definitely working for us last night, and is shown on camera from five o'clock onward, until nearly midnight."

"Thanks very much, that's perfect." At least that's one thing sorted.

Or did you think too soon, as there's a call straightaway after it.

"Hello Inspector, can you come down to reception please, there's someone to see you."

You take a swig of coffee and go straight down to find the landowner from earlier, still pacing back and forth. "He's back! He's back! So much for your detective work, why is he still free and harassing my crops! I want him charged; I want him in prison! You've been…"

"Perhaps if we took a moment to calm," you say with your hands out, "we could take a full account and I can follow this up straightaway for you." The digger wasn't

89

the killer, but he was causing a nuisance. He'd given you his address. You'll go and speak to him.

Add five minutes and turn to section 142.

Add five minutes and turn to section 142.

➤ 92

"Why did you go to the meeting and see Webb?"
"To pick up any information he might have spilled."
"And this meeting was only open to members of the Catan Cartel?"
"Yes, there's only four of us and to be honest it can be hard playing a game with six or seven people coming, you have to split up into subgroups and then you miss the gossip. Or did you mean we were determined to keep the information Webb might have had in the middle of the Cartel itself?"
"That's useful but I was more wondering what your personal interest was?"
"Oh I see. Webb came to talk to us about The Path, and I've been a follower of The Path for some time now, the whole Cartel has. I know you're going to ask, did the Cartel put us on the Path or did we all happen to choose it and it's fortuitous we all travel, and I honestly don't know. I probably would have picked it up, I am an absolute fiend for new games. I seek them out, for me finding them is half the fun, and I must have a Kickstarter arrive every week. Hmm, that's a crowdfunding platform, and there's always something you can donate to and support and hopefully receive."

To ask for Jay's views on the others in the group, turn to section 265.

To ask for Jay's views on the others in the group, turn to section 265.

⟩ To ask Jay what he can tell you about the puzzle, turn to section 238.

◄ 93

Within fifteen minutes you're standing on the street corner where the car was spotted. You know it's a red Ford Mondeo, in pretty good order, so you go into the corner shop opposite.

"Excuse me," you say to a bored shop assistant staring out of the window, "have you seen a car that looks like this?" You hold up a picture of a generic red Mondeo.

"I mean, mate, I've seen hundreds, what's it for?"

"I'm a police detective and we're looking for a car that's been driving erratically. I believe it's been swerving back and forth between lanes on this piece of road."

"Oh, right, I saw someone, I reckoned they were drunk, they went off that way but I'm not going to be able to say more than that. It's a car mate, it drives about. Unless you find it parked it could be miles away." You have to admit, he's got a good point.

You walk back out of the shop and look in the direction the assistant pointed. A long road, but there's a car park... However, a quick search of everything parked there doesn't reveal the car. You're beginning to think you've got the wrong approach for this. You'll have to head to the CCTV office and work through their data.

Add five minutes and turn to section 152.

"Mr Weald, as you might be aware a man called Harold Webb was recently killed. Did you know this man, and how?"

"Are you leading me on?" Jay replies.

"How so?"

"You know full well I knew him. He was a 'blogger', and he came to a meeting of the Catan Cartel."

"You sounded upset by the term blogger there?" you notice.

"Yes, I am. Fools, fools just trying to take my job. No education, no training, no actual jobs, just a stream of effluent on to a website, The internet has given an entire layer of idiots a job while people like myself, editors, are being frozen out, pay being cut, because no one uses us and expectations are radically reduced. So excuse my refusal to call Webb anything other than a simple fanzine creator."

"Point noted," you tell him. "However, to return to the matter at hand, you can confirm you've met Mr Webb."

"Yes, yes of course, he came to the meeting, and I was there. But I don't think a meeting in the back room of a pub has been a crime since the Gunpowder plotters were doing it."

"That rather depends on what was said," you explain.

Turn to section 175.

You might have caught Baxter Hewitt, but do you know his motive for the Path killings?

He needed money to pay off debts; turn to section 137.
He was trying to live up to his father's achievements; turn to section 176.

- He wants to launch a game he's designed from the fame; turn to section 225.
- To stop his secrets getting out, turn to section 257.
So his family will come back, turn to section 266.
Coco tells him to kill, turn to section 183.

96

"Miss Krasinski, you seem a media-savvy person, you've no doubt seen the coverage of Mr Webb's murder on the news. Do you, as someone who's met him and studied The Path, have any ideas about the murder?"

Krasinski fixes you with a look that says, I'm probably better at this than you. "I certainly do! Murder mysteries are puzzles, and I try and solve puzzles. I've been all over the news, pinned every news report I can find, and am doing the deepest of deep dives on it."

"I see, and what have you found?"

"Well, I have lots of questions for you... maybe you could learn something."

You nod back at Krasinski and inform her, "It doesn't really work the other way round, if there's a detail we're keeping from the media, we wouldn't use it except, when necessary, in a full questioning under caution."

"Ah, but just seeing you here tells me a lot, like you think another puzzle solver could be the culprit, like you don't think it was a secret lover, or a drug dealer or anything, you're here, in Sheffield."

You nod, "I think I can confirm that for you."

"Excellent. And can you give me Webb's DNA?"

"No."

"Fair enough."

Turn to section 56.

97

"Do you know any connection between Phyllis and The Path?"
"You really reckon it's the same killer? Hmm, Phyllis never mentioned anything about The Path to me, I just told her about it. I dunno if she knew anything more than I said, whether she'd ever googled it after work, she never said it unless I did. To be honest I think she was fed up to the back teeth of me going on about it, and actually she did encourage me to try and become less interested in things. Well she said obsessed about things; in case it triggered off my anger. But yeah, if I had to bet, and I do like a bet, I'd say she didn't give two shits about it. Which makes it a fucker if she's been killed by the same nutter."

To ask if he knew Phyllis Wright, turn to section 246.
To ask what they were doing at the time of the murder / arson, turn to section 24.
To ask if they have any further ideas on the case, turn to section 273.
Or return to section 218.

98

You and Robertson arrive at the Forrest's residence and ring the bell. Mrs Forrest answers, and she seems please to see you: a smile, a little wave. "Have you made progress in the case?" she asks you.

"In a sort of manner," you reply. "Mrs Forrest, how did you know Gareth Hyax?"

"He runs Puzzle! It's one of the leading puzzle magazines and he's given The Path a lot of coverage. In fact he told me Path-centric issues are his best sellers and he's always keen for either myself or 'Gato' to appear in it. Why do you ask?"

"I'm afraid to tell you that Mr Hyax was murdered today."

"Oh sweet Jesus," and she stumbles slightly, you reach out and grab her.

"Would you like to sit down; I have some questions to ask you?"

She looks at your question in shock. "To ask me?"

"Yes."

"Then right here will do."

"Did you have any recent contact with Hyax?"

"As I told you, we appeared in his periodical often."

"In the last 48 hours?"

"I... what are you getting at?"

"Did Mr Hyax try and bribe you for information on the Golden Panda? And you asked for more?"

"Ah, no, err, ah, no, look here's what happened. He knew, knows, knew The Path would make him a bestseller so he offered me a bribe, and I thought the best thing to do would be to contact the police. Tell them."

"Did you?"

"I thought I would ask for double to get better evidence, when he'd replied, I was going to go to the police."

"Really?"

"Well I'd like to see you prove otherwise!"

Turn to section 190.

"I assume you've seen the coverage of Mr Webb's murder and the discovery of his body?" you ask Hewitt.
"Yes, yes, I have. It made the morning television, although I haven't got to a newspaper yet."
"As such, what are your views on the killing? Any ideas or insights I might find helpful?"
Hewitt stifles a laugh, then grins, "Actually I do have some thoughts on it all. I think you're completely barking up the wrong tree, to use an ancient phrase."
"How so?"
"You're in the wrong place. Totally the wrong place. The killer is surely in the same locality as the victim, it will all be happening back 'on your patch' as I'm sure you say. There's nothing to suggest the killer's anything to do with Sheffield. In fact we should all be complaining you've got Gato and us on your list of people to question at all. Will you be going to the gaming groups in Glasgow for information? No, no, I did not think you would."
"You seem very certain."
"We're mostly killed by people we know, correct?"
"Yes."
"Well there we go. You're on a fool's errand and your colleagues back home will be solving it."
"Mostly."

Turn to section 148.

If you've been to this section before, please skip to the options and select one. Otherwise, read on.

There are a group of people in front of you: your team in the Serious Crime Unit. Although all are in suits and ties, they're a mixed bunch united by a strong sense of family. It can be hard being in the police, and these are the people who understand and have your back... although at your back this instant is DC Stewart, who has prepared a section of whiteboard for the team to use and is hovering with a fibre pen. A piece of theatre more than policework, it gets everyone focused on the new issue. "Okay people," you begin, "we have a murder victim. Found at 6:16 am this morning by a jogger, who handily confirms the body wasn't there before," and that information is drawn on the board. "We have a name, Harold Webb, and an age, twenty eight. We have his car, a red Toyota and yes, Steve, I'm aware you'd like a more specific model number, it's written down. We have the presumed murder weapon, so have a good start. There's a number of avenues to investigate."

To follow up the post mortem, turn to section 188. ⁴
To speak to the forensic technicians from the murder scene, turn to section 223. ⌐
To speak to Harold Webb's family, turn to section 245.⌐
To have Webb's phone examined, turn to section 12.⌐
To investigate Webb's home, turn to section 116.⌐
To follow up a possible perpetrator turn to section 274.
If you have the keyword 'TRAIN' you can turn to section 205 when you are finished here.

⌐ 101

"Would you say the main issue among the Cartel at the moment is The Path?" you ask Krasinski. She nods almost violently.

97

"We've tackled a lot of puzzles over the years we've been together..."

"How long is that?"

"...ten years. Some we've pursued ourselves, some we've pursued in competition, but nothing has grabbed all of us quite like The Path."

"How would you describe it?"

"Oooh, it's something which intrigues the mind, because you have the riddles and the text passages, all of which are really puzzles. But it intrigues the eyes, because you're also cross referencing the imagery."

"Which is..."

"No original artwork was commissioned for The Path. I'd thought of speaking to the artists, but it's all work which has been cleverly sourced and re-used I suppose you could say. Also, Gato Blanc took photographs himself, which is one reason why Sheffield has been suggested as a possible final resting place."

"You don't think starting a global mystery and hiding the answer next door to you is a little lacking?" you ask.

"No, no," and Krasinski leaps to Gato's defence. "The man is a puzzle master. A professor, to read his work is to face, and solve, genius. I'm sure the perfect answer happened to be local."

Turn to section 128.

102

"Mr Hewitt, where were you at the time of Mr Hyax's death?"

"I was where I always am, at the chemists. I mean apart from now, of course, I have had to come home during working hours so Coco and I can answer your questions."

"So you're certain you were at the chemist?"

"At that time I was taking charge of a delivery. This isn't just the FedEx man dumping off a crate of doughnuts Inspector, this is prescription medication being delivered. The people who brought it will no doubt be able to confirm they came to my pharmacy and left a consignment at that time which was taken into the shop."

You nod but have a follow-up question. "And will they be able to tell us, the delivery company, will they be able to tell us it was you?"

"Err..."

"Is there your signature?"

"No, no there isn't. I suppose the operative or whatever they are called might recall my face. But I concede they are just as likely not to remember who was there."

To ask did you know Gareth Hyax, turn to section 232.

To ask if they know anyone angry at Hyax, turn to section 36.

To ask if Hewitt has any ideas about the murder, turn to section 5.

To leave Hewitt, return to section 129.

103

"Mr Webb was working on puzzle book The Path, and that's what he was invited to the Cartel to speak about wasn't it?"

"Yeah, that's right."

"What can you tell me about The Path?"

"I consider myself expert on puzzle books, but I'm late to the party."

"How do you mean?"

"Well, you've heard of Masquerade, yeah?"

"Yes."

"So if I gave you a copy of Masquerade, and you sat down and solved it and didn't look anything up on the web or owt, you'd say you solved it, even though it's been like forty years."

"Seems fair to me," you tell him.

"Well then, I've solved Masquerade then, and lots of other puzzle books. I mean Escape Rooms are expensive, travel and all that, so I do other puzzles and when I heard The Path was coming out, I did my research, put my hours in, did some of the others."

"That makes sense. Did anyone else in the group do that?"

"Baxter did, he's done as much as possible to prepare, while Kras just did her usual thing of rocking up to it and hoping she wins. Nah, I'm being critical, she spends a lot of time cramming her head with facts for the gameshows."

Turn to section 89.

⌁ 104

"What's going on Winnie?" you ask. She looks at you with a mixture of embarrassment and shame.

She starts saying, "I tried going for a drive to clear my head. You understand don't you, this murder investigation has put me under a lot of pressure, and the same for my husband. He's always been eccentric, but I have to be the sensible one and..." she pauses. "You're not falling for it are you."

"We both know there's more to this Winnie, so what's going on?"

She lets out a deep, long sigh, as she finally gets to talk. "I thought I could end all this by finding the Panda myself. Yes, yes, I know where it is, so no one we knew could find it, but if I made a connection out there, and told them they could win it, and we'd cut them in with a small fee, and we'd get the prize money, and everything would be sorted, and our debts would go, and the murders would stop. Honestly, I did think of the murders too."

You nod in understanding, before saying, "But it went wrong didn't it."

"The person I arranged to find the Panda doesn't have the answer, they didn't get that far, because they started to blackmail me for twice the prize money! They think they'll get more if they threaten to expose us and have us sent to prison."

"I see."

Turn to section 164.

105

You take the lead and retrace your route through the woods. It's easy to see your own footprints, and Stewart's boots have a similarly recognisable tread. Both are the most recent through this area. There's a muddle of others, so you turn your attention to the foliage at either side of you. There's nothing obviously out of place, nowhere where something was thrown or some person ran off the path, and if anything is concealed here it'll need the fingertip search your colleagues will perform later to find it. Soon you've walked the whole path back, found nothing, and come to the car park. Your vehicle, and the rest of the force's cars, are still there.

As you turn you see Stewart eying you quizzically. "What was that all about?" she asks slyly. "We've literally just come to meet the forensics?" You sense she would have taken a different route, but there's no time for you to go back again, as two large vans pull up, the livery of the forensics team on the side.

"'Ello Inspector," a technician says, gets out and starts putting on his white coveralls. "You got an easy one for us today or something hard?"

Feeling you've already missed something, you reply, "Could be a tricky one."

Stewart taps her fingers on the bonnet of a car. "We might as well let forensics get on with it and start our investigation."

To return to headquarters, turn to section 100.

• 106

Sheffield's police have built a conference room which gives everyone comfortable seats, particularly those of the people doing the presenting. You've been sat in yours as you've explained to several video cameras and a lot of journalists what's been going on, and now you come to the key part.

"We urge any members of the public who can help us, in any way, to come forward. We have a phone number, now on the screen, which you can ring. If you have any information on Mr Webb or Mr Hyax, and the person who killed them, please contact us immediately in strict confidence."

You've done that a lot before, and you're happy you've delivered it with authority. Now, however, comes the wild card: questions. The people who've brought cameras for the television get to ask first, and then it would be newspapers, and then the internet. It's all going well until you point to a young man with a moustache straight from a World War One pilot's photo.

"Hello, Peter Morton, Local Mirror. Given that Mr Hyax was in the process of editing The Path when he left his room, can you confirm if this editing reveals the answer to The Path, i.e. the police now know the answer."

"Thank you, Mr Morton. I can confirm that we have no solution, Hyax's editing was of a special issue designed to spread the topic of The Path. Any solution would be a later issue."

Turn to section 167.

107

"Where were you the time of the second murder?" you ask.

Jay grins and whips his phone out. "I was going for a run, and don't you worry Inspector, I have been making sure my tracking app is on and fully functioning. So let me press this and this, and here we go." He passes you his phone. "See the times, see they're when the murder happened?"

"Yes."

"And see the tracking the phone did of my GPS. That's the route I took. Good isn't it."

"Mr Weald."

"Yes Inspector?"

"You are submitting this as evidence of where you were?"

"Why are we making double sure?"

You turn the phone round. "You actually ran to near the murder site. It's fairly close to where this route takes you."

"Oh. Oh no. That is the last thing I wanted to happen. I assure you Inspector that, despite the lack of an alibi, I did not kill anyone. Never. I really thought the phone would absolve me of any blame."

To ask did you know Gareth Hyax, turn to section 259.
To ask if they know anyone angry at Hyax, turn to section 54.
To ask if Jay has any ideas about the murder, turn to section 144.
To leave Jay, return to section 129.

108

You mimic Hewitt's tapping on the table and ask, "Do you think anyone in your group could have done the murder?"

"No of course not..." but he lets it drift off and you can imagine cogs working. "So Caroline won't be the killer because women, a vast percentage of stats say, aren't murderers. So Jay and Greg... Greg's a big bloke, some anger issues... might have raised his hands before... no I'm just musing out loud now, you'd soon drill down on to one of them. But they are here, and manifestly not back where this murder took place. No, I do declare you are in the wrong part of the country. If they're still in the country and they haven't fled. How's your French? Can't be too good or you'd be working on The Path's section seven too."

"Well, I like to make sure everything is done thoroughly. What if I told you something which will likely hit the 'news cycle' this evening."

"Go on."

"We believe we can track the killer to Sheffield."

Hewitt raises an eyebrow, "Belief isn't going to get you any convictions Inspector."

"Indeed," you reply. "Indeed."

Turn to section 231 to continue speaking to Hewitt.

⬇109

You return to your room, this time finding everything as you left it. You'll certainly be having words with whoever picked this one and booked the room here, the place certainly didn't live up to its reputation, in fact it's been living down to one. You know you can't pack your things and take your suitcase as SOCO will examine the room tomorrow, so you take a series of photos and return down to the reception to be told there's a room now booked for you at a nearby hotel. You thank the receptionist and step out into the Sheffield air. It's just a short walk through the middle of the city, and you set off. However, as you come to the end of the hotel's small car park, which is surrounded on most sides by a black wire fence, you catch something out of the corner of your eye. Turning, you think you see a figure standing at the far end watching you, and as you turn your head and focus there's a blur. Was someone there? Was someone watching you? Is your stalker, for want of a better term, still out there somewhere?

*If you go and investigate, turn to section 156.

- If you return to reception and call for assistance, turn to section 277.

110

"Do you have any further ideas about the murders?"
"Yes, I do," and he jabs a finger at you. "I heard you don't even have an armed guard around the Forrests."
"What?"
"Think about it, where is a killer desperate to solve The Path going to go when their rage grows? They'll go after the author, Gato Blanc, Forrest, they'll go after him. You should have a guy with them, a guy with a gun, a loaded gun, ready to go."
"I'll take that under advisement."
"Yeah, you do that, because if I was a killer, I'd stop faffing about with other people and go straight to the source."
"Wouldn't be great for publicity though," Robertson pointed out."
"From what you've told me, this killer is losing touch with reality."

To ask if he knew Phyllis Wright, turn to section 288.
To ask what they were doing at the time of the murder/arson, turn to section 16.
To ask if they knew any connection between Phyllis and The Path, turn to section 86.
Or return to section 46.

You've returned to Robertson's vehicle, and as she drives, she explains. "It's Gary Woods, well known to police. Multiple periods in prison, multiple theft and violence offences, but by violence I mean fights in pub car parks. There's everything in his record to suggest he'd steal a laptop, and absolutely nothing to hint he'd stab a guy to death in a different county."

"Understood," you reply.

You drive out to a suburb and soon find yourself knocking on a door. It opens, and you see the face from the camera: thin, a lip piercing which glints in the footage, and deep set eyes. He's tall too, plenty of clothing to burn.

"Oh shit, it's you," Gary gasps.

"Hello Gary. What have you been up to this time?" Robertson asks.

"Nah, nah, you ain't got nothing."

Robertson continues "I have you on closed-circuit television stealing diesel from a farm, which you used to burn your clothes. Not exactly innocent behaviour is it."

"I'll need a lawyer," he tells you.

"You will. Or you could answer some questions which would rule you out of our current murder investigation."

"Ey, what, sorry?" he splutters.

"Can you explain where you were last night, and if anyone can confirm it?" you ask.

"Who's fucking dead?" he replies. "No, no, ah, shit," and he turns round, hands in the air. "Is this a trick to get me to admit something?"

"We are pursuing a murder suspect who burned his clothes last night. You did the same." You have to admit, you're beginning to accept that Woods didn't kill anyone in your patch, the timings and situation don't match up.

"I will need a lawyer, and I will issue a statement. And that statement will show I was out robbing, cut myself, bled all over, burned the clothes, thought I'd covered tracks, in no way murdered anyone. So you can move on."

Gary Woods is not the killer, but he will shortly confess to a crime, a burglary, so note down the keyword BREAK-IN.

Turn to section 75 to continue the investigation.

⚑112

You walk down the path and see areas where once over-hanging branches have been snapped back by whoever's been down here. You can't tell much from the state of the footprints except that they carried on this way, until you get to a clearing. Two branches lead off, but you don't need to go any further as there's a human body laying curled up on the muddy soil. You don't immediately rush over, you wait and listen, watch, make sure no one is hiding in the bushes for you, but after a while and there's no sign, you head over. It soon becomes apparent it wouldn't have mattered whether you'd rushed over or waited, the body has been dead for a while. It's a woman, who standing up would be five foot tall, dressed in a once smart suit, laying in a pool of fresh blood. You find a wallet in the pocket of her pantsuit, and it confirms your fears: this is Phyllis Wright, a psychiatrist. You stand, pull out your phone, and call for support.

Once the body has been collected and forensics are on the scene, you have choices:

To head back and search Phyllis' office, turn to section 235.

To speak to Phyllis' husband, turn to section 7.

To wait and speak to the scene of crime team about their findings, turn to section 222.

‹ 113

"And yet, Mr Webb was invited to speak at the Cartel? Did everyone share your opinion of him?"

Krasinski laughs, "No, some people disliked even the hustle. I know it sounds odd for all four of us to sit here and slag off a man who we invited along, but I know none of us wanted to miss the chance to pick his brains. Why miss a chance to question him, if we could use that by letting him try and question us."

"Try?"

"Oh, none of us had any plan to share real information, or even do a fair exchange. We'd brought him in for one-way traffic, and let me tell you, that was a real disappointment. He didn't know half as much as he thought, he wasn't clever by any significant margin, he's just a media-savvy man with a minor ability in puzzles and games. We all soon knew this was a waste of time. At least I did. The others might have slightly different views, but they didn't admit to any afterwards. We all talk a lot, the Cartel, and we did have a little laugh about Webb behind his back... oh that makes me feel bad now."

Turn to section 23 to continue the questioning.

"So, Robertson, what do you have for me?"

Robertson replies to your question by holding up a piece of paper on which she's scribbled notes, then explains "We received a 999 call this morning. A man who repairs computer equipment, and I think we should go right over and speak to him. It's about a laptop..."

That brings a smile to your face, you are very much after a laptop.

You're soon walking down a busy commercial street in one of Sheffield's neighbourhoods, and you take a turn down a small road, whereupon a door is to your left in the wall. It's a thick metal door, with a sign announcing, 'Paul's PCs.' You note that it is opening hours, so you knock and the door clanks pleasingly, then you open it and step inside.

You're in a very narrow reception, with space for about three customers, a hole in a wall with a desk through which you can be served, and peering through you can see the shop disappear into the distance filled with technology.

A man in a grey shirt and black tie appears the other side of the hole. "Hello, I'm Paul, I do anything with PCs. How can I help?"

"You rang us about a laptop?" Robertson says as she holds out her badge.

"Ah, yes, excellent, I didn't know how quick you'd come."

"Nice door, secure," you say to him. "So what's up with this laptop?"

"Had a chap in here yesterday, brought a laptop with him. Seemed normal enough. Until he said he'd been locked out, forgotten the password, could I crack it open for him. Not physically, like, but hack the password. Thing is... we do help people into their computers, but guys wearing a wig which slipped as he was talking? I suddenly felt like this was stolen, and his face went white, and he looked like it was stolen, and we both snatched at it, and..." he reaches beneath the desk and produces a small laptop. "I got it, and he ran away. So if he ran... it's dodgy right? Anyway, here's a probably stolen laptop."

"Could it be your one?" Robertson asks you.

"You never know, you say," and you pick it up, whereupon you discover a sticker. A sticker promoting The Path.

* If you take the laptop to forensics for them to hack, add five minutes and turn to section 43.
  If you try and guess the password Webb would have used, if this is his, turn to section 135.
* To try and follow the escaping man's route on CCTV, add 5 minutes and turn to section 271.

·**115**

You arrange a meeting with Baxter Hewitt, and he agrees to meet you at his home and answer your questions. You arrive to find a large house in a leafy suburb of Sheffield, and there's plenty of room to park on his large herringbone drive. The front door is white plastic and there's a large and recently watered hanging basket nearby.

Baxter opens the door without you needing to knock and invites you into his house. Passing through a corridor filled with plants you come to a lounge, and Baxter sits down in his chair. He doesn't ask you or Robertson to sit, and the lounge only has two chairs, large armchairs, and there's a cat sat on the other one staring at you. The animal is big, fluffy, and doesn't look like it'll move unless you shove it. Police rules prevent you from shoving it.

"This is Coco," Baxter begins, "she'll be with me for the interview."

You're not sure whether he's serious or not, so standing, you ask your questions.

- To ask did you know Gareth Hyax, turn to section 232.
- To ask where they were at the time of Hyax's murder, turn to section 102.

To ask if they know anyone angry at Hyax, turn to section 36.

To ask if Hewitt has any ideas about the murder, turn to section 5.

To leave Hewitt, return to section 129.

116

The information you have on Webb, from his wallet and his car registration, gives you his home address, a flat on the outskirts of the city centre. You park up outside and find yourself looking up at a modern tower block. The lift appears to be working but you don't take it, instead walking up a flight of stairs that's clean and well kept. In fact the whole tower block seems in good shape, and you walk down a white walled corridor and come to room 47. You have the keys from Webb's body with you, and you use them on the door... and it unlocks and opens.

As the door swings inward you're greeted by the smell of stale coffee, then see the door opens right into a lounge. There's two tatty armchairs facing a large television, and a pot of half-drunk filter coffee sits on a table in-between. God knows how strong it was! Two mugs sit next it, but they were both unused.

You get the feeling the television wasn't used all that much as it's not the centre point of the room. Turning to your right, you find that half this lounge area had been used as what started as a small office, just a table, but, at some point, things have got out of control. The wall is covered with cut outs of things, from printouts of text, photographs and maps.

"He's even got the bits of string connecting the pins," Stewart gasps. You step carefully forward to see what all this is researching, bracing yourself for some crazy conspiracy theory and to find Webb was a tin foil hat guy... but you find something every different. There are three copies of the same book on the desk, and another completely disassembled and spread across the wall. A book called The Path by Gato Blanc.

With your gloves on, you turn a copy over and look at the back matter.

Can You Walk The Path?
We've hidden a gold panda worth £100,000.
It's somewhere in the United Kingdom.
The pages in this book are puzzles leading to real places.
Can you find the Path, the Panda, and the profit?

"Well there it is," Stewart begins sadly, "once again it's all about the money."

You look at the wall, and it's hard to disagree that someone this obsessed with something wouldn't have it connected to their murder.

"Still, could be a romantic connection, could be lots of things," you try, and half convince yourself. A few steps brings you over to the large coffee pot and the mugs.

"Was Webb entertaining before he was killed? Was it the killer? If he's been here... keep searching the house Stewart, I'll speak to the neighbours."

You step outside the flat and look at the corridor. There's a flat and an entrance door opposite, and one back down the corridor. Which do you want to speak to?

For behind you, turn to section 262.
For opposite, turn to section 291. ❧

For behind you, turn to section 262.
For opposite, turn to section 291.

❧ 117

You rush back to the park and find Robertson coming over from the other direction.
"Did you see her?" you ask.
"Who?"
"Greg was here, arguing with a woman, and they both stormed off. I can't get anything out of Greg, and I don't know who she was. Any chance you saw anything?"
"No, I was thirty seconds behind you... I had to lock the car for a start. She went that way. Let's have a look."
You spend half-an-hour, but you can't find any trace of the person Helsh was arguing with, and nobody you ask on the way round has seen her either. It's a completely dead end to the trail, so you head back to Greg's house. This time when you knock, he opens up.
"Are you following me?" he asks.
"We've had a report you've threatened Mr Forrest, aka Gato Blanc, is that right?"
Greg's mouth drops open, but he doesn't go for a story this time. You see him shrug and admit, "Yeah, I said it. I mean, threat, what do you mean by threat. I'm not gonna do it. I was just drunk and said I'd beat the answer out of the fucker, but I didn't did I, I didn't go nowhere near him. It was drunken bullshit. We all say stuff like that, right. And Baxter should know better than to ring it in. I say dumb shit all the time."

114

Well, you're inclined to believe that.

Return to section 46.

118

You ask, "Would you call yourself obsessed with The Path?"
"No, I certainly would not. I have to train for my quizzes... to be perfectly frank with you Inspector, so much of my lifestyle and income is derived from my winnings that I daren't slack in my all-out assault on the British competition scene for fear I'd have to rely on my school salary and that's not much at all."
"So your drive is financial? The Path has a large prize?"
"Is it..." she stops talking, looks at you, opens her mouth to give an answer then shuts it and promptly starts to scowl. It's almost a challenge to work out what's going on in her head, and you honestly have no idea. Krasinski seems to have taken against you. Clearly thinking of something else, she simply says, "Yes, for the money."
"Sure?"
"Yes," and her voice quavers. Whatever she's after, it isn't money. She evidently realises your conclusion because she garbles out, "It must be an addiction to winning, that dopamine hit, you know? Like when you get someone convicted. Not that you fail to get someone convicted, err... can we move on?"
You decide to do so.

Return to section 153 and choose a new option.

"Right, the killer is getting arrogant," you conclude out loud. "He's sending letters to us as well as others. First thing, which you've done Robertson, well done, is get that to forensics to see what they can find."

"Thank you, sir."

"Which leaves us having to find these clues they've put online. I want us to find the Panda's Paw and any reference to it.

"I'll get a team searching."

"Also where did this letter come from?"

"Local postmark. Doesn't mean they didn't drive here to post it but... close."

"Right, then at least we can focus on references to the local area. Panda's Paw, I want an officer looking into all the websites and blogs about The Path, anyone who's saying they have done it, about to do it, they're at risk, I want them contacted and..."

"I found it!" a detective shouts out, then says, "Oh, no sorry."

"What is it?" you ask.

"The Panda's Paw, but it's a Chinese restaurant in Manchester."

"Note it down, they seem to be using the name deliberately. Somewhere out there is a clue."

Everyone settles down and continues a deep dive into the web.

Turn to section 185 to continue.

You're stood in a meeting room that's down the corridor from the Major Crimes Unit, awaiting the woman who'd called the meeting. She was a forensics expert and has material to show you. At least, you hope she does.

She arrives promptly, but you can tell from her face there isn't going to be anything that could break the case wide open.

"Sorry," she says, pointing to the large screen on a wall, "normally I'd use that to explain to a detective what we've found, but we haven't found much. Three letters, all printed on supermarket quality A4 paper, on a common-or-garden HP printer, with no traces of fingerprints or DNA. There is very little forensically I can give you from the letters.

"I see, thanks for trying."

"We have worked something out though. The letters were posted in the same postal area as they were delivered, i.e. someone very close in proximity to the author. The sender is, at least for sending purposes, in Sheffield."

"Actually that's very helpful," you reply.

"Also, it's worth taking a close look at the text itself. I'm sure you'll find it all very helpful," and she lays three A4 pieces of paper, all covered in a special bag, on the table. You begin to read.

To read letter one, turn to section 239.

To read letter two, turn to section 240.

To read letter three, turn to section 241.

To return to your desk, turn to section 75.

When you arrive at Caroline's house you notice the front door has changed, so when you ring the buzzer, you're not surprised to hear multiple locks and chains being undone. The door opens, and Caroline peers out and around. "Just you two?" she asks.

"Just Constable Robertson and myself," you say. "Nice new door."

"Cost me a fortune, I actually paid with my own money. Got the back door done too, and all the windows checked and reinforced."

"Well," you begin to concede, "we do recommend secure homes to stop burglaries."

"And murders. Don't forget the murders."

"I won't Caroline. Can we come in?"

"Oh, yes, of course," and you're guided into the lounge. "So what would you like to know?"

To ask if she knew Phyllis Wright, turn to section 9.
To ask what they were doing at the time of the murder / arson, turn to section 296.
To ask if they knew any connection between Phyllis and The Path, turn to section 146.
To ask if they have any further ideas on the case, turn to section 26.
Or return to section 218.

A few minutes later a police car pulls into the car park and stops outside the reception door. You head out and introduce yourself. "Hello, I'm a detective from..."

"It's okay Inspector, we know who you are."

You explain the background to your call, and the uniform officers pulls torches from their kit and lead all three of you on a thorough search of the car park. Sadly, from your point of view, you don't find whoever had been in your room, in fact you don't find anyone hiding in the shadows. Nor can you prove to yourself that there was anyone there in the first place, but the officers don't begrudge coming to look.

"A new city, someone's been in your room... you've reported that have you?"

"Yes, SOCO will examine tomorrow."

"Good, in that case we'll take you to your new hotel?"

"I can't ask you to do that."

"Not a problem Inspector."

You let the officers drive you to your third hotel of the day, where you're warmly greeted by the people who man the foyer, whereupon you find yourself slipping into bed without any of your nightclothes, but they did have a toothbrush, soap and towels for you.

Turn to section 129 for the next day.

123

You ask Hewitt, "Was anyone in the Cartel, or anyone you knew, angry at Webb for any reason? Were you angry at Webb?"

"Yes, yes I was angry at him," Hewitt sneers, "he was a waste of time, and my time is precious, and he has all these readers and followers but he's all bluster. A showman. Like that movie which tries to whitewash the freakshow."

"What would you have done if he'd solved it?" you ask.

"If Webb had solved it? No one will solve it before I do. I'm going to be the best at this, mark my words. If anything all your investigation does is make The Path more famous."

"I see. Do you desire fame? Is that your end goal?"

"Fame... fame... is society interested in a puzzle solver or would I have to appear on Shag Island or whatever it's called for fame. Are there any other questions? Or are you going to be asking the same thing to all of us? I don't have time for this."

"I would like the whole group's views on the same issue," you confirm.

"Hmm," and Hewitt seems to be trying to stare into you.

Return to section 231 for more questions.

⁰124 ⁰

It's not late in the day, and Robertson offers to buy you dinner at a local restaurant. Not wanting to refuse hospitality, and with no idea of the best places yourself, you agree, and find yourself spending a couple of hours in an inner-city eatery. You discuss the case at first, and then your lives and how you've both ended up here. Robertson seems eager to soak up the lessons you've learned after years on the force, a force that work a bit differently to her patch. Then she walks you through to your hotel, and you say goodbye. She gets into her car and drives off, and you enter the hotel.

There is a receptionist there all night, and they look up and wave as you come in. It's almost as if the fact a detective in their hotel has them worried! Soon you're walking down the corridor to your room, using the key they gave you and stepping inside. You kick your shoes

off first, then walk over to the chair and dump your jacket. As you turn, you see your case on the bed...
You freeze for a moment and quickly look round the room, under the bed, then check the bathroom. There's no one there, so you come back out and go over to the suitcase, which was closed when you left this morning, and which is laying open now. You look into it carefully and see clearly someone has rifled through it and tried to put everything back.
Someone's been in your room.

Ꙩ To check the hotel's security cameras, turn to section 21.
Ꙩ To speak to reception about the incident, turn to section 109.

To check the hotel's security cameras, turn to section 21.
To speak to reception about the incident, turn to section 109.

⸱125

"Do you know of any connection between Phyllis and The Path?"
"No. None. Never heard of her. To be honest, Inspector, you should be searching her house to see if she's got a room full of notes on The Path. I assume you're counting this as a Path killing... I appreciate I'm better than a Google search but genuinely I don't think she's Path adjacent."
"Do you know any connection between Phyllis and the Cartel?"
"Why must you press this issue. I don't know if... are you trying to be sensitive and say someone in the Cartel went to see Phyllis?"
"Not at all."
"Well that's interesting. You really think it's one of us don't you, hence the three rounds of questioning... I don't

121

know what to say. I bet Caroline was seeing Mrs Wright, it sounds the sort of thing she'd do."

To ask if he knew Phyllis Wright, turn to section 213.
To ask what they were doing at the time of the murder / arson, turn to section 255.
To ask if they have any further ideas on the case, turn to section 63.
To move on, return to section 218.

☙ 126

After a good night's sleep you wake, shower and get into your suit, then come down for breakfast. There's English or continental, and you choose, take a seat and tuck in... but soon find a shadow appearing over you. You look up to find a red-headed woman of about thirty also in a suit looking curiously at you.

"Are you the inspector?" they ask you. It's now you realise you're the only person sat alone in the restaurant without a family in tow.

Holding a hand up to shake you say, "Yes, pleased to meet you."

"Excellent, I'm Detective Constable Lucy Robinson, I've been assigned to work with you."

"Pleased to meet you, and you're certainly keen. I'm not late, am I?"

She laughs, "No, no, but between here and the station there's something I need to show you, so rather than have you yo-yo about, I decided to try and catch you here."

"Makes perfect sense. Do you want a coffee or something while I finish up? I think my force are paying for it!"

She laughs again, does a thumbs up and wanders over to get herself a drink. She returns a few minutes later with a pot of tea and a mug. You finish your breakfast as soon as possible, and head out to this mystery spot.

Turn to section 70.

127

You ask Greg, "Do you have any ideas about these killings?"
"I'm happy to admit I reckon it's a traveller. Yeah, I do. And I'm not offended you're here asking all of us about it. I reckon the Cartel do all look crazy, do all look like they'd kill someone. I mean, I'm fairly certain it's not me, but I see why you're here. And the others. None of them seem like killers, but everyone says that don't they. I mean, if someone looked like a killer, you'd not meet them in, what was it, a forest at night time, right? But yeah, if I do find the solution, I ain't gonna post I done it, I'm gonna come get in one of your fucking cells and then ring my fucking lawyer to handle it. Thing is Chief, you looked into the dead guys, did any of them get close? Do you have an answer? Can you give me any clues?"
"I cannot," you reply firmly.

To ask did you know Gareth Hyax, turn to section 159.
To ask where they were at the time of Hyax's murder, turn to section 244.
To ask if they know anyone angry at Hyax, turn to 269.
To leave Helsh, return to section 129.

You ask, "Would you call yourself obsessed with The Path?"

"No, I would call the other three obsessed. I still have to train for my quizzes... to be perfectly frank with you Inspector, so much of my lifestyle and income is derived from my winnings that I daren't slack in my all-out assault on the British competition scene for fear I'd have to rely on my school salary and that's not much at all, sadly."

"So your drive is financial? The Path has a large prize?"

"Is it..." she stops talking and her eyes drift off, and you watch as her mouth curls up and down, smile and no smile, before finally her cheeks turn red. Clearly thinking of something else, she looks back at you and says, "Yes, for the money." You know that's not what she's imaging.

"Sure?"

"Yes," and her voice quavers. Whatever she's after, it isn't money. She evidently realises your conclusion because she garbles out, "It must be an addiction to winning, that dopamine hit, you know? Like when you get someone convicted. Not that you fail to get someone convicted, err... can we move on?"

You decide to do so.

Return to section 153.

Return to section 153.

⚬ 129

Gain the Keyword BLUE.

If you have the keyword GREEN, return to 46.

If you've been to this section before, please skip to the options and select one. Otherwise, read on.

The bed in your new hotel is comfortable, which makes it a shame you get up bright and early the next day and on to your borrowed desk as headquarters before most other officers are in. Soon, you present the information you have so far to the local detectives.

"Yesterday's murder was of Gareth Hyax, aged fifty-four. Same modus operandi as the killing I am here for, and same probable motive: Hyax ran a magazine called Puzzle! and had announced he had nearly completed The Path. As such I am focusing the investigation on the now definite belief the killer is stopping people solving The Path to claim it for themselves." Everyone in the room nods. "We have a number of new leads to investigate, as well as finishing yesterday's."

If you have not spoken to members of the Catan Cartel, you can do so now by adding five minutes and turning to section 212.

If you have spoken to them, you may re-interview them. Turn to section 250.

To hold a press conference for public aid, add five minutes and turn to section 69.

To follow up a call from your technicians about a laptop, add five minutes and turn to section 114.

To follow up a letter claiming to be 'from the killer', add five minutes and turn to section 3.

To follow up a report about odd traffic, add five minutes and turn to section 33.

If you have the keyword SNEAK, you may turn to section 28.

Old but still valid lines of enquiry:

To speak to the author of The Path, who's reported threatening letters, add five minutes and turn to section 40.

To investigate another report of clothing being burned at night, add five minutes and turn to section 199.

To follow up a suspicious report from an angry farmer, add five minutes and turn to section 282.

If you have the keyword LETTERS, you may add five minutes and turn to section 120.

If you have the keyword MAIL, you may add five minutes and turn to section 154.

If you have the keyword NIGHT, you may add five minutes and turn to section 191.

If you have the keyword LAPTOP, you may add five minutes and turn to 85.

130

"Are you telling me you've killed more people?"

"Quick aren't you."

"How many?"

"Five. Same as the Ripper. Good old Jack."

"And... where are they?"

"I dumped 'em, but you and your tame joggers ain't found them. I can give you details of course."

"Why?" you ask.

"I just love killing. Feeling the knife going in. I ain't got any connection between them, just they're who I saw when I was out hunting. You know how it is... I guess you don't if you ain't killed no one. Want me to draw you maps of the others?"

"Do you know who they are?"

"Nah, they dead in a hole now. I only know when they appear on the news, and you've done the naming for me."

"Please write down everything we need to find them," and you watch as he takes a chewed up biro and writes, draws, and scribbles on to a notepad. He ends up handing it to you, covered in information."

"So you'll arrest me now then?"

✎ To take the man seriously and dig for body one in a drainage ditch, add five minutes and turn to section 178. To search for body two in a woodland, add five minutes and turn to section 220.

To tell the man to stop wasting police time, turn to section 292.

• **131**

"Sorry?" Hewitt asks.

"The security cams at your shop," Robertson says turning to him, "they're broken. I asked your staff to download the footage from the last two days, and when they went over, they could see the system was down and not doing anything."

"How odd," Hewitt replies.

"You didn't know?" you ask him.

"Well it's CCTV, you only check it when something's gone wrong. We caught a shoplifter on it last week, so it must have broken since then. Maybe we didn't restart it properly."

"I see," you reply.

"But you'll see me in the shop every night working, that night was no different. Maybe something outside has caught me, on the route home, that sort of thing."

127

"Thank you," you say making a note.

"I do hope this won't count against me."

"I'll be honest," you begin, "it's a bigger issue than if you'd been taped sat there."

"I quite understand. I had better get it working again soon. Did you," and he turns to Robertson, "tell my assistant to put a call in to the engineer and get it fixed?"

"No."

"Then I had better do that. We don't want anyone else walking out with stock."

Turn to section 267 to continue.

⸵ 132

"Yeah, I guess I can tell you. I was at home working, programming app work."

You note this down and reply, "To be honest Greg, I'm not sure why that was such a secret."

"Ah, right, well I was having self-employed coffee, if you know what I mean."

You look at Robertson, who shrugs, so are forced to ask, "I don't know what that is..."

"Alcohol. I got very blitzed that night and did most of my work drunk. Thing is I know how to present a professional image for my apps and admitting you did most of it wankered isn't the way."

"Do you normally drink a lot?"

"Well, no more than the next guy. But I wasn't watching football, I was coding."

"Sounds difficult to be honest," you tell him. "Do you have anyone who can corroborate that?"

"No. I was at home on the bevvies with my laptop. I guess you could look at my laptop and note the time stamps of everything to show I was using it then."
"You would allow our team to look at it?" you ask.
"Yeah, sure thing, I've nothing to hide, like."
"Perfect."

You receive the codeword LAPTOP.

Turn back to section 166 to continue questioning.

133

You walk swiftly and gain on the woman, who is waving her arms around as if to work out adrenaline. When you get level you say, "Excuse me madam, I'm with the police." It brings her to a complete halt, and she replies, "What?"
"I'm a detective inspector investigating some incidents round here. Greg Helsh is a person of interest, and I just saw... well I'm not sure what I saw to be honest. Can you tell me what happened please?"
"I... Greg and I had an argument. Just like it always used to be. Nothing to worry you Inspector..." and she turns to go.
"Please, how do you know Greg?"
"I thought he was a person of interest?"
"Yes, yes, he is."
"But you... oh, some other crime."
"Who are you?"
"I am Greg's wife. Ex-wife, I left him. And what trouble's he got himself into? Assault again, is it?"
"Actually I'm investigating a murder."

She goes white. "I always knew it would happen one day. That's why I left. But I didn't think it would be anyone but me. Who he's killed?"

Turn to section 90.

134

You ask Krasinski, "You don't consider a shouting match a sign of anger?"

"Well, err..." and she squirms in her seat not wanting to answer. She's clearly trying not to give you something specific.

"Please," you ask sincerely, "any information could help. We don't know if this killer will strike again." Which, sadly, was very true, especially if this was all about solving The Path.

Krasinski looks at you and clearly makes a decision. "Glen is a lovely man. Lovely, salt of the earth type. Yes, he swears, he bangs tables, but that's because he's passionate. Glen doesn't need someone like you poking round and accusing him of things."

"I assure you I'm not accusing, just asking questions."

"Stupid questions."

You follow up with, "He has ever hurt anyone physically?"

"No. That's the answer, no. I don't feel threatened in his company."

"But has he ever shouted at you?"

"My parents and siblings shouted at me over the years, I daresay I've shouted at a few people, Baxter's probably shouted at the cat. Shouting isn't odd. Are you trying to say it is?"

"No."

"Doesn't mean he's murdered anyone does it. No, it doesn't."

Turn to section 251 to continue questioning.

⚘ 135

You get into Robertson's car and put the laptop in the position it was designed for: your lap. Then you turn it on. There's no reason why it would be charged, you're just hopeful, and the machine does hum into life and present a loading screen. Then it brings up a password prompt.
"You'll never get into it," Robertson tells him, "that could be set to anything. Pet, mother's maiden name..."
You don't let her finish; you instead type in what you believe Webb's mother's maiden name to be. It's rejected.
"Yeah, I'll drive us back while you play around with that if you want... good thing windows doesn't wipe after a set of failures."
"Windows, Microsoft, knows that would destroy its business because people do exactly this."
You look at the laptop and ponder what you know about Webb. A man obsessed with The Path.
You try 'The Path', and it's rejected, so you try 'traveller', and much to even your surprise the password is accepted, and the laptop home screen is revealed.
Robertson, who had started the car, now cuts the ignition and says "fuck" very loudly.
"Right then, let's see who's been speaking to Mr Webb."

Turn to section 181.

After having the door cam footage taken and analysed by your team you and Stewart wait for forensics to arrive by examining Webb's home. It's a pure bachelor pad: one set of cutlery and kitchenware in use, clothes piled up in a small bedroom ready to be washed, someone living in a one bedroom flat that was already small before they took up room with a study of The Path. In fact you don't find anything unusual except his work on the puzzle book, but as you stand once more and run your eyes over the display you find something nagging at you. There's something important you're not...

The desk.

There is a gap on the desk, and yes, there's unplugged cables leading away from it.

"Stewart," you begin, "there was a laptop on that desk. There's no computer, but there's space for one..."

"There wasn't a laptop in the car, could we have missed it in the woods?"

"It's more likely the killer took it with them... and what do you think would have been on the laptop?"

You turn and look at the wall. "Did someone kill him to win £100,000? Stewart asks.

"They may well have done."

Turn to section 216.

137

This is incorrect. Turn to section 300.

"Miss Krasinski, you seem a media-savvy person, you've no doubt seen the coverage of Mr Webb's murder on the news. Do you, as someone who's met him and studied The Path, have any ideas about the murder?"
Krasinski grins revealing perfect veneers won from a dentist. "Oh do I! Murder mysteries are puzzles, and I try and solve all the puzzles. I've been all over the news, pinned every news report I can find, and am doing the deepest of deep dives on it."
"I see, and what have you found?"
"Well, I have lots of questions for you..."
You smile back at Krasinski and inform her, "It doesn't really work the other way round, if there's a detail we're keeping from the media, we wouldn't use it except when necessary, in a full questioning under caution."
"Ah, but just seeing you here tells me a lot, like you think another puzzle solver could be the culprit, like you don't think it was a secret lover or a drug dealer or anything, you're here, in Sheffield."
You nod, "I think I can confirm that for you."
"Excellent. And can you give me Webb's DNA?"
"No."
"Fair enough."

Turn to section 165.

• **139**

You ring a doorbell and take a step back. After a minute it's opened by a man clearly expecting to receive a parcel, as he has his hands held out.
"That's not us, chief," Robertson tells him.

"Oh, sorry, what can I do to help you?"

He's six foot three with a trendy beard and slightly floppy hair. "Do you know anything about Gato Blanc and The Path?" you ask.

He scoffs, "Err... yeah, is this a joke or something?"

You explain "We're detectives, and we're investigating a series of murders connected to The Path."

"Oh. Do you know I'm the chief question setter for a number of television programmes and have more than a passing knowledge of this new paper-based trend, or is that good luck?"

You smile and say, "How do you know Caroline Krasinski?"

His smile goes. "I don't. I mean, who is that?"

"Because she arrived at your house at 10:30 pm last night and didn't leave until 5:32 this morning."

"You can't prove anything," he spurts out.

"And what would we be trying to prove?"

"Our affair. Which we're not having. We are not having an affair."

"Oh really. So why was she here?"

Turn to section 204.

140

Greg says, "Just a sec," and dives back to the other side of the room where he pulls out a huge bottle of water and comes back over, taking a deep drink. "Alright, shoot."

"What's your opinion of the Catan Cartel?" you ask him.

"Ah, good people, good people. I'm not being arrogant when I say we're a panel of experts, we really are, and we don't need arrogant fools like Webb coming in and lording it. I mean, look at Kras, she's on the telly a lot winning all sorts of shit, and Baxter's like second generation puzzle aristocracy, and I'm one of the best in my field, so yeah, we all come here and we're like the Eggheads of puzzle. That's a TV quiz show, which Kras thinks we should all go on, but the prize money hardly makes it worth it for us. Like, Kras could go on Mastermind but what's the point, a glass vase?"

"There's prizes for Escape Rooms?" Robertson asks.

"Nah, nah, I don't do it for the money, I do it for the challenge. But Kras does it for the cash, she's developed a taste for good stuff."

"What do the others do it for?" you ask.

"Baxter's got a lot to live up to. As for Jay, I think he wants to do his own Masquerade or The Path soon, I think he wants to be a setter. Yeah, imagine, Jay the new Gato Blanc. Could be good. Doubt he'd tell us the answer though, know what I mean!"

Turn to section 207 to ask him about the quavering in his voice when he said "never been locked in."

Turn to section 177 for a different approach.

141

If you have the Keyword ORANGE, turn to section 82.

You and uniform race round to Greg's house, but he's not there. You follow a tip off and find him in his local pub, but he doesn't go quietly, and has to be wrestled to the ground. He refuses to answer any questions about Mr Forrest's whereabouts.

It is only later that day, when Reginald Forrest's mutilated body is discovered, that it's confirmed you arrested the wrong person. You are taken off the case, and Sheffield's own police take charge, review the material you have collected, and arrest the right killer. You have failed Inspector.

To choose a different suspect return to section 242, or playthrough the book again and search for more clues.

142

You take the bus through the city centre and up a hill into a student district and walk along a row of terraced houses with trees all the way beside them. When you get to the target door you hear a loud radio coming from inside, a news discussion programme. There's a bell, so you ring, and a man who'd clearly just been in the shower opens the door, hair wet... he looks terrified. "Inspector!"
"Hello there. Where have you been today?"
"After we spoke, I came straight home, I haven't been anywhere. Did my alibi check out? I've seen on the news there's been a murder related to The Path. Did you think I'd done that?"
"Your alibi does check out, and news travels fast. Don't believe everything you see on television... now, can you explain why the landholder is in my reception kicking up a fuss about you still digging.
"What?"
"Have you been back?"
"No, no of course not but... I can explain it."
"Go on."
"I got talking to a guy a few days back, the kind of guy who stands at the front of the bus talking to you, and he'd travelled to Sheffield from Cornwall to try and complete The Path. So... ever since then he's been

following what I do, I might have bragged a bit. I reckon he's trying to jump in my grave, so to speak. Perhaps you could warn him off."

"What I am doing is warning you both off. I've read the introduction to The Path," and you really have, "it's not buried on private land! Something you seem to be forgetting. Stop digging things up."

You head off to speak to the other digger, turn to section 184.

143

When you come into the reception area of the hotel you see a receptionist sat facing the entrance door. She doesn't hear you come up behind her and jumps when you say, "Excuse me."

"Wait, you're with the police?" she asks.

"Yes, can you direct me to your security cameras please."

"Sure, security is through that folding counter, back through this door," which she opens with a slide of a keycard, "and then second on the left. You follow her directions and knock on an already open door. A small man is sat inside in front of a bank of monitors, most of which show corridors in the hotel, one of which is playing a football match.

"Excuse me," you say again, and he doesn't jump, instead he smoothly flicks a switch, the football disappears, and he spins round on his chair.

"You're cops, I saw you earlier. On the cameras, like."

"Can you take a look at your footage to see what happened to your murdered guest?"

"Oh, like yeah, thing is I been at it since they first said the fella been shanked, so I can send all the hard drives and stuff to your forensics, but I can show you now, like."
"Go on."
"Okay, so, look at this," and he presses some buttons and the largest screen changes to show a corridor.
"Nine in the morning. The dead guy's room is that one," and he points and leaves a print on the screen. "He'd called down to kitchen to have breakfast delivered, but before that, you can see him come out, 9:00 am, he comes out," and there a moving, living Hyax comes out of the room, looking hurriedly dressed. "We can follow him," and the young man flicks between cameras so Hyax can be seen turning a corner and then coming out of it. Like a pianist he smoothly goes through every camera and relevant piece of security tape until Hyax has left his room, rushed downstairs, through reception, across the car park, and is seen looking at a hole in the fence. He gingerly climbs through and disappears.
"And never seen alive again," the security man notes.
"That's very good. So no one ever came to his room," and you muse out loud, "perhaps the killer didn't know the room. No way to steal the phone or research..."

Turn back to section 62.

Turn back to section 62.

144

"Do you have any ideas about this case Mr Weald?"
"I'll tell you what," and Jay jabs his finger in the air, "I have so many ideas going round my head all the time it's completely disruptive and damaging. I have even booked someone to come tomorrow morning, early, to change all my locks. When I go out, I feel eyes boring into me all the

time, I feel hunted. I am sure I'll be a victim once the killer works out how close I have got to nailing this thing, I am so close, and if anyone finds out…" he's not been breathing and he has to stop to take gasps, before he looks at you in desperation. "You can't tell anyone I'm close, you can't, because if you do, they'll kill me. They'll kill me too. Promise me, promise me you won't get me killed Inspector."

"I will do my best, always," you try and assure him.

To ask, 'Did you know Gareth Hyax?' turn to section 259.
To ask where they were at the time of Hyax's murder, turn to section 107.
To ask if they know anyone angry at Hyax, turn to section 54.
To leave Jay, return to section 129.

145

You ask Krasinski, "I suppose you've pretty much answered this, but after Webb left the meeting did you have any more contact with him?"

"He gave us all his number, phone number, in case we wanted to continue the conversation, and I'll be honest I went home and stuck it straight in the bin. He knew nothing, no need to speak to him. I mean, I guess the murder stops him being the first one to solve it, but he wasn't close…" a look of realisation passes over Krasinski's face, "unless he really was nearly there, and he hid details from us like we did to him. That's something for you to pursue."

"Indeed. So no further contact."

"No, there was no further contact. I had all I needed to know."

"That's good. Do you know if the rest of the group continued their conversation?"

"No, I do not. We talk, the Cartel and I, of course, but no one's admitted to anything. Would that make them suspect number one now?"

"No," you answer honestly. "But it would be interesting."

"Okay," and you can see her making a mental note for her own investigations.

Return to section 251 to pursue another line of questioning.

146

"Caroline, do you know of any connection between Phyllis and The Path?"

"I guess I do. If she knew members of the Cartel, they're bound to have mentioned it to her. I swear Jay would mention The Path to a taxi driver all the way home. So let's assume Phyllis was seeing one or two of the Cartel as patients, that's plenty of Path related detail she'd have heard. Then let's assume the Path killer is snuffing out rivals who have nearly done it, well, obviously Cartel members have nearly done it... so... obviously they thought Phyllis had the clue. Did she leave any clue behind as to where the Panda might be?"

"I wouldn't be able to tell you if she did..."

"That's a shame. That Panda doesn't go away even if there's a killer about.

To ask if she knew Phyllis Wright, turn to section 9.
To ask what they were doing at the time of the murder / arson, turn to section 296.

To ask if they knew any connection between Phyllis and The Path, turn to section 146.

Or return to section 218.

147

You knock on the door, and Olney pulls it open, face a snarl. "You said you'd go."

"We'd like you to come down the station to answer a few more questions."

"Why? What do you think I've done?" Then realisation hits. "Do you think I've shanked someone? Shit, shit you think I've shanked someone..."

"Please come to the station, and you'll probably want to call a solicitor..."

"Oh shit, right, err, look, okay, let's be honest here for a moment. What are you accusing me of? I'll talk, just, what's the situation..."

"Will you answer some questions?"

"Yes."

"Do you know a Harold Webb?"

"No, no honestly, never heard of him. Someone's stabbed him then, have they? And I just got out and I'm the big guy in the area and... nah, nah, I didn't, I didn't, look, I can tell you where I was, cos it ain't no crime, and you can get the alibi, right, you can check it, and then you'll know, but I don't want none of this public, right? None of it. It's not a crime..."

"But you're doing a good job of not saying what it is..." Stewart interjects.

Olney leans in. "I knew a guy inside. His wife lives here. Last night I was with her, yunno, with, with," and he grinds his hips, "and this guy will kill me if he finds out, but it ain't no crime."

"And you can both prove that?"

"Well yeah, she's got CCTV up the arse. I'll be on it. Go see her. I ain't stabbed no one with anything but my meat."

"Okay that's more than enough information," Stewart says rolling her eyes.

Turn to section 51.

Turn to section 51.

☞ 148

You mimic Hewitt's tapping on the table and ask, "Do you think anyone in your group could have done the murder?"

"No of course not..." but he lets it drift off and you can imagine cogs working. "Caroline won't be the killer because women, a vast percentage of stats say, aren't murderers, so Jay and Greg... Greg's a big bloke, some anger issues... might have raised his hands before... no I'm just musing out loud now, you'd soon drill down on to one of them. But they are here, and manifestly not back where this murder took place. No, I do declare you are in the wrong part of the country. If they're still in the country and they haven't fled. How's your French? Can't be too good or you'd be working on The Path's section seven too."

"Well, I like to make sure everything is done thoroughly. What if I told you something which will likely hit the 'news cycle' this evening."

"Go on."

"We believe we can track the killer to Sheffield."

Hewitt raises an eyebrow, "Belief isn't going to get you any convictions Inspector."

"Indeed," you reply. "Indeed."

Turn to section 267 to continue speaking to Hewitt.

❦ 149

"Did you have any later contact with Mr Webb, after the meeting?"
"I bet you're thinking, Jay wouldn't have had any, if his whole technique is to sit back and let others do the pressing, but let's be honest, I'd be remiss if I let anything pass me by, so I took his contact number. It's even in my phone, look," and he waves his phone at you. Webb's number is there, but there's no messages.
"He never contacted you?" you ask.
"I must have left such a terrible impression he didn't sniff round me."
"Did anyone else take the number?" you ask.
"Oh, we all did. I bet they won't admit it, but after Greg and he had this altercation and Webb left, Caroline, Baxter and I rushed out after him and we swapped our details, you can't be too careful in letting someone get the jump on you, really can't. I assume he carried on talking to them, rather than me. The perils of being a wallflower."
"That's very helpful," you tell him.
"Oh, good, good, glad to hear things are going on the right track. I wonder if I've landed anyone in it. You probably don't admit that."
"No."

Return to section 280.

You are in a small interview room. You and Robertson sit one side of a plastic table, on two matching chairs, while opposite you Cook is sat with his lawyer. You set the recording device off and make the required statements, then you turn to Cook.

"My client has prepared a statement," the lawyer says, "he wishes this be read first."

"Please do," you reply.

"My client is being investigated for the murders of Harold Webb and Gareth Hyax. My client wishes to state he has alibis for both those murders. He has an Alcoholics Anonymous meeting which he attended at the same time Harold Webb was murdered, and everyone will remember and vouch for him. With regards Gareth Hyax, my client was at a food bank the time of the murder and will be remembered because he was thrown out for being drunk. What my client will admit to is sending you a series of letters pretending to be from the killer of said men. He sent one yesterday, and there is another currently in the post. My client wishes to apologise for his behaviour in sending these letters and has assurances from his family that they will intervene and get Mr Cook the psychiatric help he needs. Mr Cook, for his part, will engage and go along. He realises he has experienced a sharp decline in mental health and judgement and wishes to use this as a time to start recovery."

In Carter Cook, you have not caught the killer at large. But you have saved someone's life by prompting him, and others, to take a long hard look at their life and act after you gave them a caution.

Gain the Keyword LOST.
Return to section 129 to continue the investigation.

"We're investigating the murder of a Mr Harold Webb. Did you know the victim?"

"Yes, I did." Krasinski finishes her reply and waits for a long and awkward pause, before adding, "Oh, do you want me to talk about him? You don't have more 'questions'?"

"Sorry, yes, please tell us what you know."

"Okay, this is my first time being interviewed by the police. Not what I expected. Okay, Webb is, was, is, was a big name in the puzzle blogosphere. He has a considerable following among hardcore puzzlers, such as the kind you'll find in the Cartel, and in casuals, who make up the bulk of his views on YouTube and the like. I've never been tempted by social media, but I believe he was a pioneer of this content on TikTok and the like. Made a big name."

"Popular then?" you follow up.

"Undoubtedly."

"I detect a tone in your voice?"

"Oh, you noticed it, I didn't expect you too. I can respect the man's hard work, but he was insufferably arrogant. If you've not solved a puzzle and you listen to him, he'll make out he's a god. If you have solved a puzzle and listen to him, he'll make out he did it three weeks ago and you're too slow to bother with. As I said, most listeners were casuals, overawed by an apparent ability."

Turn to section 264.

You head over to Sheffield city centre's main CCTV hub and find a recently re-equipped unit that work in close contact with the police. There's so many screens you think you're in a sci-fi programme, and a team of expert operators ready to help you.

As you sit in a guest chair just to the right of the operator, a coffee is handed to you, and you show the make of car you're after; a red Ford Mondeo acting erratically.

"Alright sir," the lady with the buttons and little joystick begins, "let's have a look."

She brings up the footage of the location and time that was called in... and there is a red Mondeo moving from one lane to the next and back seemingly at random. It drives past the camera and off, but the operator smoothly flicks screens to the next camera, and you watch as it moves. A little zoom and you can make out, at least you think you can make out, the face of Winnie Forrest, although any emotion is lost.

"Hang on, what's she doing?" you ask as you realise.

"She's driving round and round this circuit..." the operator explains, "and look, this is a live feed, she's still out there going..."

"Great," you say as Robertson pulls her radio out and sends a squad car to intercept and stop the vehicle.

To go to where Winnie has been stopped, turn to section 227.

You call over the next member of the Cartel. She's short, thin, and exceptionally well-dressed, managing to combine labels with actual fit. She has a handbag that probably costs your monthly salary, but despite this she sits down and smiles at you very sweetly, almost excitedly. She brushes loose brown hair back behind an ear.

"Hello, I'm the inspector, and you are…"

"I'm Miss Krasinski. Caroline Krasinski."

"And how old are you?"

"I'm 29."

"And what do you do?"

"Oh, well that's the question isn't it."

"Is it?" you ask to prompt a reply.

"It's very complicated."

"What do you put on your tax form?" you ask her.

"Oh, that's easily, I'm a primary school teacher." She notices how you turn and look at the handbag in surprise. "Well, that's the thing, I earn most of my money from quiz shows. I've been on them all, on normal TV, on cable, and I win a huge amount from magazines and all that. You've probably seen me before," and she grins.

"It's certainly working for you," you reply.

- To ask, 'Did you know the victim?' turn to section 35.
- To ask, 'Were you at the meeting?' turn to section 233.

  To ask, 'Where were you night of the murder?' turn to section 294.
- To ask, 'Was anyone angry at first victim?' turn to section 6.

  To ask, 'Do you have any ideas about murder?' turn to section 138.
- To ask, 'Have you won many kitchen knives?' turn to section 73.

  To return to the Cartel, turn to section 212.

On the way back to the station you make a call. It's a quick one, but it's to the team at the office to request the relevant rights and pull up the financials of the Forrests. The letters you've retrieved make it clear they're deep in debt, but what exactly is going on? Debt can, sadly, be a huge catalyst for crime.

On return to the station you sit yourself at your desk and ring the publisher. They provided your team with Forrest's Sheffield address, but had they been entirely honest?

"Hello there, just following up a call one of my colleagues made, she's DC Stewart."

"Oh hello detective?" the voice is gender neutral and waits for a name.

"Yes, Inspector. I was hoping you could tell me more about The Path. How's it selling, what reception has it got?"

"There are many fanatical fans determined to walk it," the publisher says with a trace of frustration.

"I sense that's not all."

"Sales are low. Very low. It's fanatics or nothing."

"And does Forrest know this?"

"Which one."

"Sorry?"

"Mrs Forrest has taken over communications, we deal solely with her. She's the only one who knows we're in danger of trying to recoup the advance from them, let alone pay any royalties."

"I see."

You had better speak to Mrs Forrest.

Turn to section 76.

You break into a run and come up behind Greg but know it's dangerous to just tap a massively angry man on the shoulder, so you call out. "Greg, Greg stop there please, Greg this is the inspector, the police, stop there."
It takes a moment, but Greg's big strides slow, and he turns confused.
"Inspector? What... what are you doing there?"
"I should be asking you the same thing Greg. What was this? What happened here?"
"I... where did you come from. What did you see?"
You're assuming Greg had a violent argument with the woman, but you don't know that for certain.
"Tell me what happened Greg?"
Greg looks at you, and you can see, despite the anger in him, there's a part in the minutest piece of control telling him not to confess anything to the police. You can see, on his face, the moment he seizes on an excuse.
"Some bitch shouted at me for kicking the trees."
"Sorry what?"
"They've planted these new trees, saplings or whatever, and I was in a right mood, angry, I've had a few cans, so I went for a walk, and I got annoyed, and I kicked the trees, and this busybody has a go at me, and we have a back and forth and then we moved on. Stupid, but just some fucking back and forth. You know how it is."
You don't, but there isn't much you can do here.

To find Robertson turn to section 117.

You stride across the car park towards where you thought you saw 'them'. You pass a series of parked cars and start moving out of the lit areas and into the shadows, with your eyes not adjusting as fast as your feet move you. As you reach the site of the… well whatever it is you saw, you see it again, movement in the corner of your eye, a snap turn of your head and a blur. This time you run after it, covering ground quickly and soon finding yourself in a completely dark area of the car park, but the shadows seem extra dark in the area before you.

"Police," you announce, "show yourself," and you focus on the extra dark spot, as your eyes struggle to resolve what you're seeing. It could very well be a human trying to hide, crouched down behind a car.

You step forward, your eyes continue their war, and you hold a hand out in front of you. There's a torch in your suitcase, but you didn't think you'd need it, nor can you take it until it's been dusted for prints. Which leaves you…

Suddenly your world explodes in light and stars, and you feel something very painful on the back of your head.

Turn to section 34.

You follow up by asking, "Did you speak to the Webb?"
Baxter replies, "As before, I am going to clarify your definition with that."
With no hint of frustration you ask, "While you were reading his blog, and I presume his social media…"
"Yes."

"... did you exchange messages with each other. Online contact?"

"A limited amount. I have no respect for the man but it's a fool who doesn't pay attention to his rivals."

"So you considered him a rival?" you ask innocently.

Baxter snorts. "I see what you did there... and yes of course, we are all rivals even if our background and ability is widely different. The thing about Webb is he got so far and was nakedly trying to use other people to go the rest of the distance. It turns out Webb didn't know half as much as he claimed online, and he was hoping the Catan Cartel would take him the rest of the way. I think we all knew it, but I suppose if you're trying to keep traffic," and his words drip with contempt, "to your website, then you're under pressure to solve it."

"Are you under pressure?" you ask.

"It's a race. All travellers are. But not from Webb."

Turn back to section 267 to continue.

158

"Jay, in your dealings with Webb, did you learn of anyone, or believe anyone, to have reason to kill him?"

Jay holds his palms up and answers, "No, I don't know why anyone would kill anyone honestly."

"You're designing a game about a murder?"

"Can we stop talking about my game! I do not want to talk about my game! This is not an Expo!"

"Sorry to have touched a nerve Mr Weald, you did mention your game first."

"We're not schoolkids."

Moving on. "Did you know of anyone who was angry with Webb?"

"That's more understandable, at least from my headspace. I suppose you could say we are all angry at Webb, because he's a rival traveller on the Path and he's already making money off his social media talking about it. I wouldn't be good in front of camera, but Webb's YouTube was racking up the views, and the income. I think we'd all like a piece of that. And yes, I know you expect me to say Greg was angry, and I guess Greg was angry, but honestly, Webb was a pathetic sort of man who'd come to probe us, and I'm glad Glen kicked him out."

You allow your surprise to show in a raised eyebrow. "Speaking of Greg…"

Turn to section 71.

159

"We're now looking into the murder of Mr G. Hyax, does that name mean anything to you?"

If anything, the fact there's been another murder seems to calm Greg. "Oh yeah, I've had my eye on him. No, shit, wait, that makes me sound guilty. What I mean is, he said he was close to finishing, so everyone's been dreading anything he posts. He tweets, we all look through one eye and breathe a sigh when it's just another advert for his shitty magazine." A pause. "You said he was dead? Alright, I ain't gonna slag a dead man's magazine. It was a fine magazine. But I guess he ain't gonna solve it no more is it, so… not too terrible for the living, I guess. I mean you gotta be real haven't you, we're left here, no traveller's gonna lose sleep over him."

To ask where they were at the time of Hyax's murder, turn to section 244.
To ask if they know anyone angry at Hyax, turn to 269.
To ask if Helsh has any ideas about the murder, turn to section 127.
To leave Helsh, return to section 129.

160

There's three sets of muddy footprints leading towards you as you travel the opposite direction down the path. You feel you can rule out the recent, partial steps of the jogger. Which leaves two others... a killer and a victim? You're hopeful as you wind through the wood, trees full of green leaves and the much smaller but brightly coloured plants all around you and raise an eyebrow as you come to a fork in the path. The jogger has come down one route... so you follow the pair of footsteps along and into a second clearing. This one is much smaller, circular, and is big enough simply for the single vehicle, which is parked here, a red Toyota still wet from the drizzle.

One of the doors is open...

You look closely around you, noticing the footprints you've followed start at the doors of the car. A driver and a passenger, and it's the driver door that's open. You walk carefully so as not to disturb anything which lets you take a peek into the car, which is empty of people or more corpses.

You pull your radio out and call in the registration number. A moment later, and you get a reply.

"This car is a red Toyota?"

"That's right," you confirm.

"It's registered to a male called Harold Webb and... just a second Inspector."

"Of course."

"Yeah, thought I knew the name, Mr Webb was reported missing this morning."

Unconsciously you turn and look at the path you've come down. Sadly Mr Webb might not be missing any more.

It's time to return to headquarters and set up, turn to section 100.

✦161

"Do you think he wasn't killed for the puzzle, or just that none of the Cartel would have done it?"

"Ah, I'm convinced no one here killed him. Someone down there might have, there's travellers all over the place. But if I didn't kill him, and I'm stressing this right now," he points at you, "if I didn't kill him, then no one in the Cartel did."

"What makes you so sure?"

"They're all so soft. Kras is a woman, so she's out, Baxter's whatever kind of man has more interest in his fucking cat than people, and Jay's just timid. None of them have the balls to fucking kill a guy. So, if it's Path people you'll have to find who else Webb was talking too, cos it's no one here. You can rule me out too. I'm not fucking soft, if I was going to kill someone, I wouldn't need to lead them into a wood, I'd just batter them where I found them. Wouldn't use a knife either, got these fists God gave me. All these screens, your hiding from fists. People are soft, we've lost the art of backing up the bollocks you're saying with some presence. I reckon I should stop talking there."

Turn back to section 166.

Your phone rings, and you see the name of the caller: "Winnie Forrest." Tapping it on you say a silent prayer that this isn't something else the Forrest family have got themselves involved in.

It will go unanswered.

"Hello Winnie, what's..."

"Inspector, Inspector, you've got to come here right now, my home right now, get here as quickly as you can. I need you now, now, bring people with you, get here." With that, the phone goes off.

Well, what else can you do. You hail Robertson and you dash to her car, and soon you're speeding along, with a call going out to a uniformed unit to meet you at the residence.

"On a scale of calm to 'we get to go full-on foot down', how anxious did she sound?" Robertson asks you.

"Full-on foot down," you reply calmly, and the car accelerates away. Soon you come to a screaming stop in a suburban street, leap out and go rushing over to the front door of the Forrest residence which is swinging open in the wind.

"Winnie?" you shouted in through the door, "it's the police..."

A squad car with backup screeches to a halt behind you.

Turn to section 242.

The farmer is surprised when you ask to walk back to the farm, and you let him lead the way as you restudy the route you've just come down. You were fairly certain you saw something of great interest. After a short walk you reach the farmyard, where a tractor is just being started up and driven away.

"Would you like a tea then?" the farmer asks.

"That fire," you begin, "had a strong smell of diesel. I wondered if they took any from the vehicles or your storage?"

"I'm afraid I wouldn't know," the farmer replies sadly.

"Ah but would that?" and you point up to a small black device attached to a wall.

"My son put that up," the farmer explains, then stops. "Oh, the camera."

"Is it real and working?" Robertson asks.

"Yes, yes, it is, my son works here with us, he does it. His, err, computer is attached, I think. That's inside but we'd have to call him in if we're going to do anything with it. He's password crazy, I'd never get it on for you.

"Can't be too careful. Perhaps if you call your son, we can have the tea while we wait?"

"Good idea."

Turn to section 171.

It's later. You're sat in your car, which is parked on a road overlooking a bowling green. Nobody is playing, but someone is stood by the grass, someone holding a large leather bag. You watch, closely, as this figure walks back and forth, before a man appears and walks over to her. They speak, and the man points to the bag. The figure, Winnie Forrest, puts the bag on the ground, the pre-arranged signal. As you leap out of the car and say "go, go, go" into your radio, figures emerge from the bushes on the bowling green and chase the now fleeing man. He doesn't get very far before an officer barrels into him from the back, bringing him down in a perfect Rugby tackle, and soon the man is cuffed and being taken away. You go over to Winnie, and a leather bag which just contains a pile of magazines, and check she isn't shaken by the experience.

"So, Winnie, what have we learned from this?" you ask her.

"To stop any little schemes and go to the bank asking for debt relief."

"Yes, yes, exactly that. If we cross paths like this again I will have to charge you with something."

Turn to section 39.

165

"But now you know that, Miss Krasinski, perhaps you could follow its logic for us. Say I was interested in people in the Catan Cartel. Do you think anyone in your group could have committed this murder, or be involved in some way?"

Krasinski nods to herself, and it's evidently the first time she's considered the concept. "I would say... well I watch a lot of true crime don't I, and I would say I would have no idea would I. Often a killer is someone everyone's totally surprised about when it happens. There's no way I'd know if the group were involved," and she shudders, "we'd all be just as surprised as anyone else wouldn't we."

"Well, yes, my job does involve a lot of surprises…"

"That's no help for you is it. Hmm, do I know anything… I'm going to be honest; I don't think I can rule anyone out. Honestly, I don't. Why wouldn't it be any of them? I think we're all a bit weird in our ways, aren't we," and she finishes by looking at you and grinning. She really is enjoying the drama of all this.

Return to section 153 to continue your questioning.

166

Greg's face is bright red, and he's clearly trying to keep his emotions under control. As you tilt your head and look behind him you can see the rest of the Cartel looking over confused. This is not their first brush with Greg's temper, and you decide a pause might be good.

"Would you please fetch me a drink please," you say to the member of the pub who's been hanging about in the room to monitor how their premises was being used for this strange meeting. A minute later a coffee arrives for you, and although it's hot, you sip it. Greg seems to have calmed down after practicing a rudimentary breathing technique for calming, as if he knows he has this temper and has been trying, slightly, to control it.

"We gonna finish this?" he asks, sounding desperate to move on.

You nod yes.

- To ask, 'Did you know the victim?' turn to section 289.
- To ask, 'Where were you the night of murder?' turn to section 272.

To ask, 'Do you have any ideas about the murder?' turn to section 4.
To ask, 'What can you tell me about this puzzle?" turn to section 268.
To ask, 'What do you do for a living?' turn to section 68.
To return to the Cartel, turn to section 212.

167

The press conference goes on until all questions are answered, then you bring it formally to a close. The camera operators start to shut things down, the press rises and prepares to leave, and you leap to your feet and rush over to the woman who'd been pinning your mic to you.

"Turn this off," you order.

"Yes, yes, I have, what's got into you?"

"Can you stop everyone leaving please."

"What?"

"Block them for five minutes."

Then you rush back to the desk you'd been sat behind and snatch up your notes, hurriedly looking through.

"What's wrong?" Robertson asks.

You now cycle through the slides. "That bloke. Morton. The Mirror. He asked about the papers being spread around being edited... but how. We've not told anyone have we? That's never gone to the press. That's not gone beyond the CID room. How did he know?"

"Jesus, you're right, no, no, you're right, we've not told anyone."

You both turn back and look at the room of people trying to leave.

"So we grab him, yeah?"

"Yes, we do."

159

You walk over to Peter Morton, who is in the middle of the pack.

"Mr Morton, stop for a second please, I have a question," you say, and he disengages from the scrum and comes back." As he does so, you nod at the organiser, and she lets the rest go.

Turn to section 202.

﹙ 168

"Was anyone in the Cartel, or anyone you knew, angry at Webb for any reason? Were you angry at Webb?"

"I wasn't angry at the man," Hewitt replies dismissively, "he was a waste of time, and time is precious, but I'd rather find out someone had failed to solve the puzzle than find out they'd solved it. I suppose... was I angry... no. No."

"What would you have done if he'd solved it?" you ask.

"It didn't come to that did it," he replies brusquely. "Besides, no one will solve it before I do, but you asked about the rest of the group. Were they angry... I guess you'll have to ask them. I don't tend to worry how they're feeling because they will be disappointed by me anyway. Besides, don't you have to know someone to be angry at them?"

"Do you?" you ask genuinely interested.

"Maybe. I don't know. Ideas appear and leave don't they, I don't know where that came from. Something to think about certainly. Anyway, are there any other questions? Or are you going to be asking the same thing to all of us?"

"I would like the whole group's views on the same issue," you confirm.

"Hmm," and Hewitt seems to be trying to stare into you.

Return to section 267 for more questions.

169

You ask Jay, "Do you have any thoughts on the murder?"
"I hadn't... I mean... " and he looks caught out, like a schoolboy who'd not done the homework, "I saw a report on the news, but I didn't start to puzzle it out or anything. Should I have done?"
"No reason to."
"I can only assume, if it's puzzle related, like, you must think if you're here with us, what must have happened is he either solved it and someone killed him to silence him, or he fooled someone into thinking he was close, and they killed him for the same reason. Be a shame if he hadn't found the Panda, bragged, and got murdered."
"Would it not be a shame if he had found the Panda and was then killed?"
"Oh," and Jay looked even more guilty, "yes that does reflect back on me doesn't it."
"Do you think anyone in the group did it? Could do it?"
"No, to be honest I think they all had him lined up for press and coverage when they did find it. Even Greg would have given him a call and said get me and the Panda on your channel. We're a shameless lot, we really are."

Turn back to section 293.

170

You open the book carefully, and find something very interesting... wait a minute, you're not supposed to be reading this section, there's no link to it in the book. Please don't read pages until you're sent to them, or you will spoil the mystery.

171

Two Yorkshire tea bags later and you're enjoying your usual brew along with Robertson and the farmer. He's just offered you some bacon sandwiches when the old wooden back door opens, and a man walks in. He looks exactly like the older farmer would have done twenty-five years ago, and it's almost spooky. You have your hand warmly shaken, introductions are made, and you all cram into a small office where the younger farmer has set up his own office. It's incredibly neat and well organised, and you watch as the young man types possibly the longest and most complicated password you've ever seen into the machine. It works.

A few mouse clicks later, and there's a black and white video stream of everything the camera caught the previous night, complete with time stamps... and yes, there is a figure who is very much not supposed to be there, sneaking about the farmyard and stealing a small amount of fuel.

When Robertson leans in you raise an eyebrow, and in one key shot the intruder turns and his face is clearly visible on the camera.

"I know him..." Robertson exclaims, "I know exactly who that is."

Turn to section 111.

⸋ 172

"Have you tested your puzzles out on the rest of the Cartel?" You consider it an innocent enough question to lead on to other things, and are fascinated to see Jay go completely white, as if the blood has drained out of his face and into his feet. He starts fiddling his fingers and hands together, and his leg starts jiggling.
After a long pause, in which he knows he has to say something, Jay squeaks out "What do you mean."
"You said you design games; you've tried them on the Cartel?"
"No, no," he squeaks again.
"Why not?"
"I, err…, I… would prefer not to discuss my writing process."
"It's not of direct relevance to the murder, but it's interesting to me…"
"I…" and Jay is frantically scrabbling around in his mind for an answer to this, before you can see in his eyes how he alights on an excuse. "I'm just an old British eccentric who doesn't want to share his work with his rivals before it's published."
"You think the Cartel's members would steal your work?" you ask flatly.
"Err…" and Jay realises he's only got one answer to this. "Yes, yes I think they would."
"Interesting."

To answer further questions turn to section 293.

"Caroline," you begin, "where were you the night or Mr Hyax's murder?"

She goes bright red and looks at the floor. "I was with my boyfriend. We were doing couples stuff..."

"Ah I see. And is there anyone besides your boyfriend who can support this alibi?"

"Oh, he'll definitely remember!"

"That's not what I meant. As a romantic partner he's not automatically to be believed."

"Oh, I see!" Krasinski's eyes look into space as she starts thinking. "I seem to remember his neighbours saw us as we were saying goodbye, I think they would vouch for us both, but again, of course, please, I don't want any of this getting out into the press. They would ruin both our lives. You know what the press is like!"

"Yes, yes, I do. But perhaps don't leave yourself open to that?"

"Yes. Well. You can't stop love Inspector."

To ask, 'Did you know Gareth Hyax?' turn to section 248.
To ask if they know anyone angry at Hyax, turn to section 208.
To ask if Caroline has any ideas about the murder, turn to section 48.
To leave Caroline, return to section 129.

174

Later that day, your DCI looks up from the papers you've given them, a summary of the case so far.

"And we don't have any idea who this figure is, just the clothing?" they ask you.

"That's correct, we know they left Sheffield railway station, but we don't know anything after that. However, they have a bag on them which is big enough for most laptops so it's possible they have it."

"And this thing about the puzzle. The victim was obsessed with a puzzle book written by a man in Sheffield."

"Yes."

The DCI leans back. "I don't know how much you're going to like this... but bearing in mind everything you've learned so far, and having spoken to the constabulary in Sheffield, I have arranged for you to travel up there, work with them, and pursue the fleeing presumed killer."

"Okay, that's a surprise..."

"They've already made progress and are keen to meet you and go on. They've assigned a detective constable to assist you."

"That's fine sir, absolutely fine."

"Of course, you need to tie up loose ends here first, but get that done quickly and be off as soon as you can. A hotel room awaits.

Note down the keyword TRAIN.

If you have the keyword GAME turn to section 205. If not, return to section 100 to continue your investigation locally.

⚑ 175

"Did you, despite your suspicions of bloggers, speak much to Mr Webb at this meeting?"

"I said hello, nodded, made sure I did enough to have been invited, but I left the main body of discussion come from others. They were very keen with their questions, but Greg got very annoyed by Webb's either lack of knowledge or lack of sharing and brought the whole thing to an unpleasant end. Greg felt personally insulted."

"You were more of an eyewitness than a participant then?" you offer.

"Yes, exactly," and Jay points at you. "I hoovered up any information offered but did little else. I certainly didn't start planning to murder the man, or whatever you think I might have done. Webb might have had many flaws, such as being a showboating junior school level writing talent, but I didn't see anything that would make someone kill him."

"Did you learn anything? About The Path I mean?"

"Did I pick up any clues? I suppose... I can't honestly break it all down, everything goes in and becomes one mass of knowledge. I didn't come home and regard it as a complete waste of my limited life, so perhaps I did."

Turn to section 234.

176

This is correct, give yourself twenty points and turn to section 300.

177

You place a cross next to the name of Greg in your notes as you raise your head up to call him over, but you feel a tap on the arm from Robertson. She hands you a handwritten note she's just made:

"Checks from the team at HQ have come in. Greg Helsh is the only member of this group with a criminal record. A record for assault."

You nod at her. "Greg please?" you say out loud.
A man stands up, and he's six foot three and wide. He has thick blue jeans that have faded, a flannel shirt, and a large, long beard. He couldn't have looked more like a cartoon lumberjack if he'd come over carrying an actual tree.
"Alright?" he says as he sits down. He's fidgeting, looking at the floor, the walls, anywhere but you and Robertson. His hands are the size of plates and he's constantly wringing them.
"Hello there, Greg, how do you pronounce the second part?"
"Hell-Shhh," he explains, and seems to relax a little as you'd hoped.
"We're here to discuss what you know about Mr Harold Webb and The Path."
"Right yeah and nothing else right?"
"That's correct." It isn't. "How old are you, Greg?"
"Forty."

To ask, 'Did you know victim?' turn to section 19.
To ask, 'Were you at the meeting?' turn to section 182.
To ask, 'Where were you the night of the murder?' turn to section 186.
To ask, 'Do you have any ideas about the murder?' turn to section 203.
To ask, 'What can you tell me about this puzzle?' turn to section 103.

167

To ask, 'What do you do for a living?' turn to section 221.
To return to the Cartel, turn to section 212.

178

There is a man in plastic waders which come up to his
waist. They're green, and his top half is wearing the sort
of weatherproof jacket you could walk up a Welsh
mountain in and survive. He's moving carefully along a
drainage ditch filled with so much rainwater no one can
see the bottom... or perhaps that's due to the thick,
muddy liquid rather than the quantity. The man, who
works for the police and has a perfectly functioning desk
he'd like to go back to, has a glorified pole which he's
using to probe the bottom of the ditch. This has been
going on for several hours, and you've been stood in the
drizzle watching. The man in the waders has searched the
area Dealve gave you, and everything alongside it, and
looks at you.
"Honestly, Boss, I don't think there's a body here, I really
don't."
You are tempted to agree with him.

To search for body two in a woodland, add five minutes
and turn to section 220.
To tell the man to stop wasting police time, turn to
section 292.

179

As you scan the room you notice something on the
bedside table. Not only a packet of nuts, dry roasted, but
a mobile phone. You walk over and note the make but

also slip it into an evidence bag. In doing so the phone activates, and you discover that Hyax has no password or fingerprint identification on it. Anyone could literally open his phone and start reading.

Normally you'd recommend everyone have security on their equipment, but with the killing recently probably occurring after someone interrupted Hyax and drew him outside, you click on the recent messages the phone received...

...and you find something. The last message the phone received was from an unknown number.

"Come to the Car Park. It's XoX. I have intel for you."

Which was pretty much what you expected and is something you would have followed up had you not seen the message that came in before that. The message is listed as coming from Mrs Forrest and reads:

"What you're offering isn't enough. There's a deal to be done, but I need twice that sum. You'll sell sooo many copies of the magazine when you 'find' the Panda..."

"Robertson," you say without looking up, "we're going to need the car."

If you have Keyword ALPHA, turn to section 15.
Otherwise turn to section 98 to speak to Mrs Forrest.

• 180

"You can't just sneak up on people!" he shouts at you, and you move yourself physically, so the spade is now behind you.

169

"I'm a detective inspector and I've been invited to this field, whereas you..."

His face falls at your reply. "The police? He went to the police. I want to field a complaint; the landowner chased me off!"

"Did he touch or threaten you?"

"Err..."

"No, he did not. So why are you here with a shovel?"

"I'm walking the Path!" There's a worrying element of religious zeal to his voice.

"You believe the solution is somewhere in this field?"

"Err... well sort of. I don't really know, exactly, I've got a load of possibilities, but I'm kinda just brute forcing it. Did you know if you took a metal detector across this field, this place we're standing buzzes?"

"And obviously you asked the landowners permission to start digging."

"Better to ask for forgiveness and all that."

"Can you tell me," and you pause a little, before saying, "where you were yesterday evening?"

"What?"

"Where..."

"I was on my shift last night."

"And what's that for?"

"Bus driver. Err, if this is an alibi for something my bus'll have loads of CCTV."

"I will check that out, but that's a good answer from your point of view. However, you cannot dig anywhere else in here without speaking to the landowner. It is against the law."

To return to the office and check with the bus service, turn to section 91.

It takes you a while to start ordering and filtering the data to be found on Webb's laptop, as he was highly organised, just to a system in his head no one had ever heard of before. There's a great deal of emails, including all communications organising Webb's in-person meeting with the Catan Cartel, and that all checks out.

What really gets your attention, however, is a messaging system. Called WhatsApp, it allows people to communicate via cell phone numbers, and yes, there's chats started from Webb with the members of the Catan Cartel, but nothing untoward is to be found in those accounts, which all relate to the Cartel's phone number. No, what catches your eye is a contact simply labelled 'Mystery' and the short exchange that followed.

Mystery: Webb, I have information for you.

Webb: Who is this?

Mystery: My identity is a secret till we meet.
Mystery: This is a 'burner' phone. Don't try and find it.

Webb: What information?

Mystery: I believe you have nearly found the Panda. Nearly but not quite.

Webb: I'm not going to give that away to a random stranger.

Mystery: you haven't found it because it doesn't exist.
Mystery: Gato Blanc / Reggy Forest is a fraud. Meet me and I'll show you.

Webb: You have information showing Forrest to be a fraud? There is no answer.

Mystery: Yes, I do. Bring your data and I'll show you. Forest is a fake.

Webb: Come to my house. It's…

Mystery: I know where it is.

You look up at Robertson and think out loud. "The killer didn't lure Webb with a solution, he lured him by playing on Webb's failure. 'Bring your data', the killer thought, knew maybe, that Webb was close."

Turn back to section 129 to continue your investigation.

182

"Why do you go to the Cartel?"
"Ah, it's good isn't it, meet up with your peers. Yeah, it's not totally my scene, but I like the folks and it's close enough."
"How would you describe the Cartel's scene?"
"Well-written puzzles, spoken puzzles, board games, stuff like The Path, it's all good, all good but it's not specifically what I'm all about."
"Okay, what's your scene?"
Greg's eyes light up and he stares straight at you. "Escape Rooms. Fucking Escape Rooms, I love them, I'm one of Britain's top escape room experts. Just lock me into somewhere and let me puzzle it all out to escape. I done a-hundred-and-fifty-seven and never been locked in

172

once. Yeah, I'm a king and I love it. The clock ticking, the adrenaline rushing, you talking to your team mates, running about, trying, yeah, it's great. Maybe I should have done bomb disposal or something. Not that I'm saying it's same, like, yunno."

"How long did a-hundred-and-fifty-seven take you?"

"Years. I done American ones, Australian ones, never tried a European one cos they all in funny languages, sorry can't say that can I, other people's languages."

You think you've spotted something.

Turn to section 207 to ask him about the quavering in his voice when he said "never been locked in."

Turn to section 140 to ask about his views on the rest of the group.

Or turn to section 177 for a different question.

183

This is incorrect. Turn to section 300.

184

You step off the tram and go into the reception of a hotel. Although you intended to head straight up to a room, a smiling receptionist calls out, "Can we help you?"

"Hello, I'm with the police," and you show your badge, "I'm just visiting someone to ask some questions."

"Of course, anything we can do to facilitate."

"Thanks. Have you seen anyone coming and going with a shovel?"

"Oddly," the receptionist replies, "we have."

You don't take the lift but nip up the stairs and are soon knocking on a door. It's opened by a rotund man who doesn't look at you, just waves an arm and says, "Do bring my room service in."

"I'm a police inspector..." and that gets him looking up, in great alarm. "Can you please tell me where you've been today?"

"Err, can I have a lawyer?"

"You can, but you'd have to come down to the station and, let's be honest, that doesn't make you sound innocent does it. So, why don't I come in and you can explain why people have seen you with digging tools."

"Err... I'm trying to follow The Path. It's this fantastic mystery..."

"I know what it is. I know you've been digging up other people's land and following a fellow traveller around. I'm here to remind you of the law. I'm not going to caution you, but I am telling you if I have any more word about either of you, you're both ending up in a cell."

"Yes sir."

To return to headquarters and leave this red herring behind, turn to section 75.

185

You're all searching for the Panda's Paw when your phone goes off.

"Hello?"

"Hi Inspector, I have some information for you about the letter you dropped in to us," the forensics expert on the other end explains.

"That's excellent, and fast."

174

"Yeah, well, here's the thing, we quite quickly found a thumbprint on the envelope, and were able to get DNA from it. We got a match too, because a chap called Carter Cook was done six months ago for drink driving and we still have his DNA on file, so they match."

"Good job," and you slap the desk in pleasure.

"Yes and no sir, yes and no. We have Cook's address, you can go speak to him, but six months ago Carter Cook was employed as a postman. It's entirely possible he actually put the letter into your bag today."

"Don't worry about that, we'll get it all checked."

"We'll keep going on the rest of the letter, thought I'd start you off early as it were."

"Perfect."

A postman?

"Everything alright?" Robertson asks.

"I'm going to need the number of the local Royal Mail sorting office; we have a question we urgently need to ask them."

Turn to section 84.

186

"Mr Helsh, where were you the night of the murder?" It was a standard question, something you'd ask all people of interest in a murder case, and sometimes it produced a very bad reaction. This was one of those times.

"You're not pinning this on me!" Greg shouts. "No, no, you said it was questions about the murder!"

"If we could speak calmly Greg, that is a question I'm asking everyone in this room and a good few people beyond. Perfectly innocent, helps us complete our

175

picture. Asking is in no way a reflection of how the investigation is going. Okay?"

"You sure? Why should I trust you?"

"An alibi rules people out. So, give us your alibi, everything's safe."

"Yeah, yeah I see."

A pause.

"I still want you to answer it," you add.

"Oh, right. Do I need a lawyer? Is this a lawyer sort of thing?"

"Most people don't need a lawyer to give us an honest answer to what they were doing at a certain time."

"Hmmm. I suppose not answering makes me look more guilty. I mean, a little guilty. Yunno what I mean."

"That's not for me to say, Greg."

Turn to section 243.

Turn to section 243.

✦187✦

In the reception of Sheffield police headquarters a phone starts ringing and is swiftly answered.

"Hello, this is..."

"Sorry, sorry, this is the police, I know," comes a woman's voice. "I don't know who else to ring, but I need to speak to officers investigating the Path murders."

"The Path murders?" the officer who answered says.

"Yes, that's what they're called, the..."

"Sorry madam, I was just thinking out loud. I know exactly who to put you through to."

Your phone rings, and you hurriedly answer it.

"Inspector, I have a woman who's keen to talk to you about the case."

"Put her through please," you ask.

"Hello? Hello?"

"Hello there," you begin, "I'm the inspector investigating this case. How can I help you?"

"My name is Phyllis Wright, and I'm a private psychiatrist. I work in Sheffield. I need to speak to you please."

"Certainly, we can facilitate that. What's it about?"

"Can you come to my office? Can you come now?"

"Yes, yes I can, but what..."

"The killings, the killings you're looking into. Get here fast please." She hurriedly gives you an address before the phone is slammed down.

Turn to section 60.

188

Although the receptionist offers to show you through to the morgue, she and you know it's just a courtesy: sadly you've travelled this way too much. You find your own path round, knock on a door and step into a white room filled with shiny metal instruments and doors. The man in the middle turns round. In a thematic white coat and shiny metal clipboard, forensic pathologist Dr Garret Viklund greets you. He has blond hair cut short against his head, and a pair of wire rimmed glasses that have elastic round the back of his head as well as loops for the ears.

"Hello Inspector, Constable," Viklund begins. "A pleasure to see you. I assume you have come about today's work?"

You see Stewart wince at Viklund's dispassionate view of the murder victim, but assume you have to have a slightly different view of the world to perform autopsy's every day of your working life.

"Yes, what have you found?"

"Well, I have performed a thorough examination. The man might be in his late twenties, but he has the liver of a fifty year old, although I suppose alcoholism is the least of his worries now. However there were no alcohol or drugs in the man's system when he was killed. He'd eaten a meal shortly before, lasagne, had no time to digest. Let me sum the body up thus: you are familiar with the myth that Jack the Ripper cut people with such skill he must be a doctor?"

"Yes?"

"Well Mr Webb was killed by the opposite of that. Death was definitely from catastrophic blood loss following many stab wounds, but there is no talent or skill or planning: whoever killed him just began randomly stabbing the victim wherever he could. There are defence wounds on the arms and hands, and penetrations of varying depth around the whole torso. The weapon was an eight-inch blade. Definitely not self-inflicted. Punctures to most major organs, but again, these were not sought out, just a panicked, borderline psychotic attack. Given the state of the body I would place the murder between 8:00 and 9:00 pm last night. He was laying, deceased, in the woods overnight.

"Thank you, is there anything else?"

"If I had to play detective, I'd say the killer hasn't done this before." Viklund smiles, and it's not pleasant.

"Good to know."

You return to headquarters, turn to section 100.

Greg Helsh is currently in custody for domestic violence (thanks to you) and cannot be contacted at this moment.

Return to section 218.

You ask, "Do you and Mr Forrest have alibis for today?"

"Us? We would never murder anyone!"

"Nonetheless, where were you today?"

Suddenly Mrs Forrest's agitation calms. "Actually that's easy. We were playing bowls and dining out with the club. There must be thirty witnesses to us. They'll see you right. Nothing to do with us, if anything we should be scared there's a serial killer on the lose trying to solve The Path!"

"Regretfully, it does seem like that's happening," you admit, before walking back to the car. You pull out your phone and look up the Sheffield Bowls Club and call the chairman.

"Hello there, I'm an inspector working in Sheffield. Can you answer a question for me please?"

"Yes of course, anything to help the police."

"Did you hold an event today, lots of bowling, a meal, that sort of thing?"

"That's correct, Detective."

"And were the Forrest's present for all of it?"

"Oh yes, two of our resident authors, yes, they were there. Reginald won all his games, but Winnie seemed very distracted, like she was thinking about something. I can however confirm they were with us all day."

"Thank you very much."

Return to section 62.

191

You and Robertson take a drive out to the home of Miss Krasinski. She lives in a terraced house that's far taller than it is wide, and you know she's not home because the expensive car she won and drives is absent. That's okay, because you're not here to ask her questions, just questions about her.

You walk beyond Krasinski's house to her neighbour and press a buzzer. After a while a tall, broad woman opens her door and looks out at you confused. "I haven't ordered anything."

"Hello," you begin, "I'm with the police and I'm hoping you can answer a quick question for me."

"Is it about my kids?"

"No."

"My brother."

"No, your neighbour Caroline Krasinski."

"Right, that's right, what's the question."

You show the woman a date and ask, "Was Caroline Krasinski at home all that evening, do you know?"

That gets a snort of derision. "Nope, she wasn't. She went out. She's always going out alone at night and coming back alone. Dunno what she gets up to, but it can't be no good, if you know what I mean. Surprised she's even bothered having a bed in her place. That it then, is it?"

Note down keyword SNEAK.

If you have heard the name Mr Hyax turn to section 129. Otherwise turn back to section 75.

"That's a lot of research, The Path must mean a lot to you?"

"Yeah, nah, I gotta be honest, I want it for the money and the fame. I got a lot of bills to pay, don't earn much anymore, and The Path would shift me a shitload of apps. And let's face it, when you know you're good enough to solve it, why wouldn't you try? That Gold Panda's worth a hundred grand, and I'd be on telly more than Kras, so... yeah you bet I want to solve it. Especially at the moment. I gotta be honest, if I did solve it, I might have to split it with Kras, cos yunno, they'd put her all over the telly and I think the cancelling bastards might have a go at me, so I'd cut her in for like twenty-five per cent."

"Why Kras, sorry, Miss Krasinski and not Mr Hewitt and Mr Weald?"

"Cos she's a woman I guess." You can feel Robertson trying to control the expression that so desperately wanted to appear on her face. "I don't think it's bad to talk about money. I'm honest yeah, I want the money, no shame in that. All the others want it, but I bet they never say it."

Turn back to section 166 to continue.

The door doesn't move. You give it ten minutes of complete silence from within and go back down to your car. Sitting inside, able to keep a clear view of the stairwell, you ring Robertson.

"How's it going Inspector?" she asks.

"Badly. Mrs Wright isn't here, even though she sounded desperate to talk. Have you had any contact from her? Any follow-up calls?"

"Nothing I'm afraid Inspector, not a word."

"Alright, please keep me informed if anything happens."

You ring off and decide to take a walk. You move along the parade of shops and go down the alley which leads to behind the building. There's cars parked here, with a small road looping round and out, as well as large yellow dumpsters. With your years of experience nagging at you, you quickly look in each dumpster, but there's nothing suspicious. If Phyllis had a car, would it still be here? You're about to ring Robertson to have someone look Wright's car up when your phone goes, and the DC is ringing you.

"Inspector..." Robertson says.

"You sound worried?"

"I had someone ping Wright's mobile. She's not at the office. She's in the wood behind the building..."

Turn to section 261.

194

"Toby Olney?" you ask to the man who's just turned off the main footpath into a garden. You'd travelled to Olney's current home address, been told the man had gone out, and found your eyebrows raising at the perfect timing of him coming to find you. It's obvious he's just been to a barbers: prisons aren't known for dying people's hair bright green, as his just has been. He wears a new pair of jeans and has black trainers, as well as a sweatshirt with a well-known metal band on it. He is also highly unhappy to see you.

"What do you want? You the police?"

You smile as you ask, "Why would you assume that?"

"Two people in suits at my door, you ain't my parole officer so you'll be the police trying to harass me. Yeah, harass me."

You reply, "Sorry if you feel harassed, I was hoping you could answer a few quick questions to rule yourself out of a recent incident. Just a few minutes and we'll all move on."

"Do I have to answer?" he asks.

"Not at all. You can say nothing, you can ask for a lawyer, anything you want."

"Oh right," he says as if he's suddenly solved the Gordian knot, "and if I don't say anything I look well guilty don't I. Alright, go on, what's the question?"

"Can you please tell me where you were last night? Ideally between 6:00 and 10:00 pm?"

You've been a detective who's risen through the ranks, so you know when a person's face turns to genuine shock, and how they're lying when they look away from you and mumble, before going, "Went to the cinema. New Marvel thing. Superhero shit. Right, piss off the pair of you."

You and Stewart step aside and Olney goes into the property and slams the door behind him, then you return to your car. After a moment's thought, you pull your phone out. There's one cinema in this area, and you ring them up. "Hello, do you have any Marvel movies on at the moment?"

"Err, no, no, we don't."

"Thanks."

You and Stewart exchange looks. It's obvious Olney is lying, and you have a good case for hauling him into the station to find out why. But is this a waste of time? Is there any reason he's connected to the murder?

To question Olney, turn to section 147.
To return to headquarters, turn to section 100.

195

Jay opens his door, and it's clear he's been crying. His eyes are red, cheeks stained, and he goes into his lounge and flops on a chair.

"Are you okay Mr Weald?" you ask.

"I'm upset. Okay, I'm upset, and who wouldn't be... but I'm being a terrible host, please go and help yourself to tea and come back in a moment. I'll try and get myself composed."

You go into the kitchen and find five empty vodka bottles on the side, which seems a sizable number all things considered. When you return to the lounge with a drink made for Jay to calm him down, he seems to have regained control.

Okay, what do you want to ask me? I know what one of them will be.

To ask if he knew Phyllis Wright, turn to section 288.
To ask what they were doing at the time of the murder / arson, turn to section 16.
To ask if they knew any connection between Phyllis and The Path, turn to section 86.
To ask if they have any further ideas on the case, turn to section 110.
Or return to section 46.

You begin with, "Regarding the meeting between the Catan Cartel and Mr Webb..." but Krasinski interrupts you.

"Yes, that took place."

"Okay, thanks, we're certain of that but..."

"It was in this very room. We all sat along that table like we were interviewing him for a job, or Dragon's Den or something. Looking back it wasn't very friendly, but we did spend a while on musical chairs before Baxter decided to stick us all down one side. Webb didn't seem worried, he seemed like he'd put up with it in order to get information out of us."

"I see, thanks for the description. Why where you at the meeting?"

"I'm the most successful member of the Cartel," Krasinski said beaming.

"How does that translate into coming to the meeting?"

"Well, I presumed I'd be the one he'd recognise, and expect to see, and I find it my responsibility to always be the face of the Cartel."

"So you've mentioned them on television?"

"More than a few times! I think we're famous, at least in puzzling circles, thanks to my winnings. I bet people give a sigh when they check winner's lists in their magazines and see me."

To ask about the others in the group, turn to section 37.
To ask more about The Path, turn to section 14.

"Mr Weald," you begin, "where were you on the night of Mr Webb's death?"

He sidesteps the questions and asks, "Does that ever work?"

"How do you mean?"

Jay explains, "In all your years in the police force, when you've asked, 'where were you', did anyone ever answer, 'at the victim's house stabbing a knife into them.'"

"Generally speaking if they don't have an alibi they say no comment," you answer honestly.

"Ah, and I am supposed to give you an alibi now, that wasn't just a friendly question, this is where I prove I was nothing to do with it."

"I suppose, 'Jay', that is exactly the current situation."

"In that case I shan't say no comment, I shall tell you the truth, I was out for a run. I don't know if you can tell my BMI from that distance and with myself in this excellent coat, but I can run a mean 5K, and a damned sight more. I do all the park runs round here and one day I might try the London marathon, although I'd have to do some charity thing to be allowed in and that just looks hassle."

Turn to section 59.

Caroline is forced to wait a whole five minutes past the time you had arranged to meet her, which means the tea she has made you is already going cold because, for reasons outside a police investigation, she'd poured the drinks before you'd arrived. Nonetheless, she welcomes you into her home, and you settle down on to several very comfy sofas which she explains she won from a magazine for over sixties and had to get some elderly friends to collect. Which, you assure her, won't be getting her into trouble with the police.

"Are you making any progress?" she asks, her voice catching slightly in her throat.

"All the time," you say, although you're not sure if you believe it.

"What did you want to ask me?" she asks keenly.

To ask, 'Did you know Gareth Hyax?' turn to section 248.

To ask where they were at the time of Hyax's murder, turn to section 65.

To ask if they know anyone angry at Hyax, turn to section 208.

To ask if Caroline has any ideas about the murder, turn to section 48.

To leave Caroline, return to section 129.

◦ 199

"So what's this about burning clothes?" you ask Robertson.

"Funny thing really, we had the call with the barrel first, that was attended and identified as connected to your case, but later we had a separate call, from a farmer, saying he'd chased off someone causing damage on his land, which questioning revealed to be a pile of burning clothes. So, might be worth checking, see if it's connected?"

"Okay, let's swing by."

There follows a twenty-minute drive as you leave the centre of Sheffield and move into the country beyond, and you smile as seeing the hilly landscape and an area new to you. Soon, however, Robertson turns her car up a trail, you bump along the tracks and reach a farmyard. You've heard a lot about vast agricultural economies of scale leading to huge fields and similar machines, but this farm is like something out of the 1950s, or even the thirties.

You've barely had time to get out when a man in a well-worn waterproof coat comes over.

"Good day sir!" he begins, "I assume you are the police?"

"I'm the inspector, and this is Constable Robertson."

"Excellent, excellent, come with me, you'll be okay without wellies, come with me and see this."

The farmer's keen to get on, so you follow him through some buildings and across the edge of a field before you find yourself at a metal gate between the field and the road. There's what looks like some fly tipping, and in a bathtub is a pile of something that's now burned.

You walk closer and get close. It's definitely burned clothing, but SOCO would have to examine it for more information to be gleaned.

"When did you find this?" you ask.

"Overnight, someone burning it here yesterday evening." You nod and ponder. There are definitely footprints leading away, and you're sure you saw a security camera back near the house.

- To follow the footprints, add five minutes and turn to section 230.
- To follow up the CCTV footage, add five minutes and turn to section 163.
- To dismiss the incident and return to headquarters, turn to section 75.

She opens the door fully and you step in. The paint brush is carried out of sight and the homeowner returns with her phone, and she pulls up the app that's been monitoring her door cam.

"You're lucky, it saves forty-eight hours of material. So what time?"

"Start at 5:30 pm?"

She presses a few buttons and holds the camera so you can see it. A press and the footage fasts forward, until someone arrives. Someone, because while you can make out their height, build and clothes, you can't see their face. This newcomer is invited in by Mr Webb, whose face is visible briefly, and another fast forward until the pair come out and leave together. Again, you can't see a face, but you can get some clues.

The time checks out. That looks likely to be the killer.

Turn to section 136.

"Do you think your father would have travelled the Path?" you ask Hewitt.

"My father?" he says shocked.

"Yes, puzzle 'royalty'," you said, a phrase and inclusion which struck you as odd. "Would this have interested him?"

Hewitt's face grows darker, and the edges of his mouth curl down. "My father solved Masquerade before anyone else but didn't go public because he was happiest working for the Times. Did not want to interfere."

"So you've got big footsteps to follow in then," you reply innocently enough, assuming there would be no way of checking the previous claim.

Hewitt begins to glare at you. "My father has nothing to do with your investigation of some nobody and I would ask you to leave him out of it. I do not need to match my father's achievements to be somebody, I am a success in my own right."

This was not what you were expecting. "Of course, my apologies, I'd simply thought you'd want to talk about him more."

"Well you got that wrong. Let's hope the rest of this 'police enquiry' goes better for you, or you won't get far at all."

"Indeed." You've got plenty of notes to make in your book.

Turn to section 231.

٭ 202

"What can I help you with?" Morton asks and looks at you keenly.

"If you don't mind me asking, you seemed particularly interested in matters relating to The Path."

"I suppose you could say that," he replies. "I'll save you probing, I have some interest in the murders but local interest in The Path is high, seeing as the creator is local, and I felt I could play on that audience with a good headline."

"I see."

"Not, I grant you, something that'll help you much. You want to catch the killer."

"At the moment, Mr Morton, I want to know who told you Hyax was editing his magazine when he left the room."

Morton doesn't look alarmed, but he doesn't answer quickly either. Then finally he says, "He's a magazine editor. Lucky guess."

"It wasn't, you were certain. How did you hear of this?"

"Well Inspector, you're an inspector aren't you, I don't have to tell you. Let it just be said that I have a source on the police force, and I would go to prison before I told you who it was." He smiles, enjoying this far too much.

You look at Robertson. "Do you know this man?"

"Yes."

"And will he go to prison first?"

"Oh yes, he's a stubborn sod."

"Then, luckily for you, I have a murderer to find. You can leave."

Morton walks smugly off.

Robertson asks you, "What do you want to do about this?"

To leave this line of inquiry behind, return to section 129.

To have a search run through the email system, add five minutes and turn to section 77.

To give everyone working with you different briefing notes and see what happens, add five minutes and turn to section 237.

To interview everyone working with you, add ten and turn to section 215.

* 203

You ask Greg, "I assume you'd heard about Mr Webb's murder before you got the call asking you to be here?"

"Yeah, I saw it on the news, and I already recognised it was him. Instant. I thought fuck, who's he pissed off, cos he wasn't the type to ever kill himself, far too full of himself for that, so yeah, I knew he'd done it. When you gave me the call, wasn't surprised. Know you'd be doing your job, following leads. Man speaks to group about hundred grand prize, dies soon after, yeah, yeah, that'd do it."

"And what do you think about the murder?"

"Yeah so, I think you'll agree with this, people are mostly killed in romantic attachments, aren't they? Husbands, lovers, stalkers, all the crazy stuff love makes you do, that's right, isn't it?"

"I think you might be mistaking the old adage you're mostly killed by someone you already know."

"Oh yeah that's probably it. But Webb, he's a fucking prick, he's bound to have pissed loads of people back off in your patch. Jealous exes? Mad girlfriends? Bad boyfriends? Stuck it where he shouldn't? I reckon that's your main target once you run out of stuff here."

Turn to section 256.

ᴐ 204

A door opens and Caroline rushes in, speaking at a hundred-miles-an-hour. "What's wrong, you sounded so worried on the phone..." but the man who opened the door just pointed to a space behind where Caroline was now standing. A space where you and Robertson are sitting in his lounge.

She turns.

"Oh fuck."

"Would you like to explain what's going on?" you ask her.

"I didn't kill anyone, I didn't…"

"Kill?" the lover almost squeals.

"… but you must have checked my alibi for the murder and discovered… I lied about the alibi. I'm in a relationship with this man here, and the night and time of the murder we were together."

"If I'm going to believe you," you tell her, "I need to know why this is so secret?"

"He sets puzzles for television shows. Shows that I've won. It's how we met but strictly speaking I shouldn't appear on them in case he's given me the answers."

"And has he?"

"Do I need a lawyer?"

"No. I'm investigating two murders not prize money. But I would caution you not to lie to the police again. This is a waste of time that could have been avoided.

Note down the keyword SNOOKER.

Turn back to section 129.

Turn back to section 129.

○ **205**

You'd like to think you'd only need to pack a light bag and you'll have this murder solved within a few days, but you're also realistic. That's why you arrive at the local railway station with a large suitcase filled with work clothes, casual clothes and all the equipment you now can't live without. You're not travelling in your work suit, as it's later in the day and you'll be heading straight to your hotel room.

The train is only five minutes late, and you sit yourself at a table with four seats facing it… but you're later than rush hour and there's just you with the table all to yourself. This gives you room to spread the notes you've made out and review them.

Time passes, and you're soon stepping off the train on to the platform on a sunny summer evening. There's stairs up, stairs down, and you're carrying your case out into the fresh air. A turn of the head reveals a parking area filled with taxis to your right, and you hire the one at the front to drop you at the hotel. You've picked a place in the city centre, and while you could have walked you didn't risk being the detective that got lost on your first day in the city!

The receptionist puts on a good show of being pleased to meet you, gives you a key with a yellow plastic tag, and you take the lift to your room. It's small but perfectly functional, with a single bed, armchair, a smaller chair and a table, and a TV. It will be a good home for you the next few days. For now, time to sleep and meet your contact in the morning.

New Rules: for you, Inspector, the clock has started ticking. From now on certain sections will ask you to mark off five minutes. Keep a track on the chart at the back of the book, and when you would tick off a time which asks you to turn to a section (50, 110, 135), turn immediately to that section. You may return to the line of inquiry that prompted the five minutes later for free.

Turn to section 126.

₹ 206

Robertson doesn't have enough reason to hit the sirens and break the speed limit, but she does quietly get you to Greg's house in a record time. You leap out and ring the bell, then look in through the windows while you wait. When there's no response you check the side gate, find it unlocked, and slip round, but your search reveals no Greg, or any clue. You get back to the front and Robertson is ringing once more.

"Nothing," she tells you. You look at the drive, and there's a car there.

You turn and nip next door, ringing that, and it's opened a short while after by an elderly couple who have come together.

"Hello, we're the police, have you seen Mr Helsh go out at all?" you ask.

"Yes," they both answer together.

"Which way, how fast?"

"He walked over that way, very fast for Greg, doesn't move that quick these days."

You say thank you and walk off in that direction. You can't hear anything, but maybe if you went round the corner, you'd see something. The path and the road continues, but there's a narrow piece of path that splits off at ninety degrees, the sort of route you'd have to leave your car to travel down. On that basis you walk down the new path, winding your way between houses before you hear it: raised voices.

You recognise one and break into a run, and suddenly you emerge into a playing field. Greg is walking away, muttering obscenities, and a woman is going in the opposite direction, face all red. Evidently there's been some trouble here.

To catch up with Greg, turn to section 155.
To catch up with the woman, turn to section 133.

"Can I come back to one point."

"Yes."

"You said you've never been locked in, which would constitute losing correct?"

"Yeah."

"Is it true you've never been locked in?"

"What?"

"Your voice, when you said that. What's the real situation?"

"Do you know?" Greg asks turning to Robertson, "Does he know?"

"Detective Constable Robertson looked up any background logged by the police of Cartel members. I did the same thing too. I happen to know you have a criminal record for assaulting the staff of an Escape Room when you failed to leave."

Greg's mouth drops open, but he eventually forces out, "You said this was about the murder."

"It is. You have a history of violence. A man you've argued with has been killed. It's a fair line of questioning."

Greg's face goes red, "I'm being set up, I'm being set up, you fuckers, I didn't kill no one, I didn't."

"Who knows you failed the Escape Room?"

"What?"

"Roughly. Do the Cartel know?"

"No they don't, and you can't tell them. They think I got drunk and had a fight in a pub. That's what I told work, and they fired me. My wife knows the truth. But that's it. You can't tell no one."

You explain, "I have no intention of doing so unless you become a likely suspect."

To ask other questions turn to section 166.

You ask Caroline, "Do you know anyone who was angry at this second victim, or anyone who had a reason to kill him?"

Krasinski whips a pencil up off the side table and starts to chew on it, then says excitedly, "I've been thinking about this. If Webb and Hyax were connected by The Path, I find it unlikely that someone who wasn't involved with The Path did it. If I were you, I would be looking solely at travellers, people who want to solve the mystery not just people who want the reward. Let's face it, if I wanted a hundred thousand pounds quickly, I would just go rob someone, not try to solve an impossible set of riddles. So yes, I expect everyone who feels they have a chance at The Path is aggrieved at the pair of them saying they had nearly finished it. You're after a traveller... oh that's why you came to the Cartel. We were all suspects..."

To ask, 'Did you know Gareth Hyax?' turn to section 248.
To ask where they were at the time of Hyax's murder, turn to section 65.
To ask if Caroline has any ideas about the murder, turn to section 48.
To leave Caroline, return to section 129.

⁋ 209

"We understand that Mr Webb arranged a meeting with you, with the Catan Cartel, to discuss The Path. Is that correct?" you ask.
"Yes, yes, it is," Hewitt replies.

"Did you attend that meeting?"

"Yes, yes, I did."

"Would you like to give me your account of it?" You lean back into the hard, upright wooden chair.

"He contacted us, although I'm not sure which of us. A message went out, do we want to do this. There was a general feeling among the group that it would be a good idea and he was invited. Again, I don't know who actually set up times and place, but nonetheless we met, had a fruitless conversation and all went home."

"Why did you go?"

"Me? I gather every scrap of information about The Path, because you never know, you never really do, but it became apparent he hadn't got any information we hadn't already come to. If I'm being honest, and I suspect you want me to be, tempers were fraying by the end at the waste of time for everyone except him, and we were all glad to leave.

To ask about the others in the group, turn to section 278.

To ask about The Path, turn to section 258.

To ask a different question, turn back to section 267.

210

"Did you, despite your suspicions of bloggers, speak much to Mr Webb at this meeting?"

"I exchanged pleasantries with the man, kept a voice in the conversation, but I left the main body of discussion come from others. I think, looking back on it in my mind as I sit here, that Baxter led the grilling, while Caroline answered any questions, and of course there was Greg who got very annoyed by him and brought the whole thing to an unpleasant end."

"More of an eyewitness than a participant then?" you offer.

"Yes, exactly," and Jay points at you. "I hoovered up any information offered but did little else. I certainly didn't provoke an argument or look desperate for any secret information."

"Who do you think did the latter?"

"I am sure you, as detectives, can work it out from what I said! Or do you need everything spelt out?"

"Sadly, Mr Weald, a courtroom and a jury do need everything spelt out."

"Of course, of course, in that case, Baxter. I assume he'll tell you I looked disinterested, which I did not, but impressions can be wrong, can't they."

"More often than not Mr Weald."

"Jay, please. Not Jason."

Turn to section 149.

211

Winnie screams as she is cuffed and taken away, as you start a detailed search of the house to see if she's left her husband's body there or taken it somewhere else to hide. However, you can't find any sign.

It is only later that day, when Reginald Forrest's mutilated body is discovered, that it's confirmed you arrested the wrong person. You are taken off the case, and Sheffield's own police take charge, review the material you have collected, and arrest the right killer. You have failed Inspector.

To choose a different suspect return to section 242 or play through the book again and search for more clues.

* **212**

Robertson directs you off a tram at the required spot, and you find yourself walking down a couple of side streets.
"Good thing the pubs open promptly," she says to you, as you stop in front of one.
"Why so?"
"The Catan Cartel regularly hire the back room here, and they only agreed to meet if we used their home."
You raise an eyebrow, "What did they expect to happen if they refused?"
"Well, they didn't anticipate we'd turn up at all their workplaces and ask for a chat I suppose," and she laughs to herself as she opens the pub door. You step inside, and find an old-style boozer that, if it had been in a film, would have been filled with tobacco smoke. Not now, but the carpets were still sticky, and the barman still nodded almost violently for you to head on back and not keep spooking the clients, some of whom were already desperately trying to avoid eye contact.
You take the lead and walk round into a wooden panelled back room, where four people sit sipping, before eyeing you up sceptically.
"Hello everyone, I'm the inspector, and I believe you're ready for me to ask you all some questions?"
They all nod.
"We," the woman begins, "all read the book and solve the puzzles, which we call walking the Path, to find the Panda."

- To talk to Baxter Hewitt, add five minutes and turn to section 267.
- To talk to Greg Helsh, add five minutes and turn to section 177.
- To talk to Caroline Krasinski, add five minutes and turn to section 153.
- To talk to Jay Weald, add five minutes and turn to section 280.
- To finish questioning and head back to headquarters, turn to section 75.

● 213

"Mr Hewitt, did you know of the psychiatrist Phyllis Wright?"

"Are you implying I'm mad?" he snaps back.

"There's lots of reasons someone might know her, without being a patient."

"And how's that spelled? R I G H T?"

"There's a W. Wright."

"I don't recall ever reading anything from her about The Path.

"And you didn't know her in any other capacity?"

"Are you implying I'm mad?" he asks again.

"So, firstly, seeing a psychiatrist does not make one mad, Mr Hewitt, and secondly, I know you have been seeing her."

"Oh, I see. Well I'm not mad. I just don't want to broadcast the fact I have needed to speak to someone and have been speaking to her for three years. I had a breakdown when my mother died, and if you broadcast my visits to her I will sue you. I am not mad."

"Of course you're not. I appreciate it's a touchy subject."

To ask what they were doing at the time of the murder / arson, turn to section 255.

To ask if they knew any connection between Phyllis and The Path, turn to section 125.

To ask if they have any further ideas on the case, turn to section 63.

To move on, return to section 218.

To ask what they were doing at the time of the murder / arson, turn to section 255.

To ask if they knew any connection between Phyllis and The Path, turn to section 125.

To ask if they have any further ideas on the case, turn to section 63.

To move on, return to section 218.

⋆ 215

"You really want to bring everyone who might have seen this data in, and ask them if they leaked it?" Robertson asks.

"I want to be somewhat subtler than that, but essentially yes."

"Right. I'll get a list drawn up…"

It takes a long time, hours you could be spending on the murder case, but you go through everyone who might have seen the relevant material. First you find out if they did admit to seeing it, then you probe if that information has been sent on anywhere… including to a journalist. As the interviews go on you sense a growing truculence among the Sheffield detectives, including one exchange that stings you.

"You've come over here, asking for our help, sitting in our office, and you go accusing us all of telling people shit? What makes you think you can sit in judgement of us, eh?"

You have no answer, and after everyone has been spoken to you have to admit to yourself you do not know who leaked this information, in fact you're not second-guessing yourself it was ever leaked at all. With the station turning against you, it's time to return to the murders.

To leave this line of inquiry behind, return to section 129.

• 216

You are sat in a briefing room several hours later. You finished your search when forensics arrived, and they took over. As you suspected, there was no unknown DNA on the mug, whoever came simply didn't stay long enough for coffee to be poured. There was a power cable for a laptop plugged into the wall, but the other end hung loose on the floor.

The real breakthrough, however, came courtesy of Webb's neighbour. With the image you have of the guest and presumed killer who left with Webb, you've been able to get a description of the clothing worn, including a hat and hoodie. No face, but the clothing has been enough for your team to pull up all the CCTV footage they can in the town and actually follow the pair to a car, and then the car until it turns off the road into the wood. The hoodie man is now the prime suspect, but what takes you further happens when a very excited detective constable holds up a remote control, points at the screen of the briefing room and says, "Watch this."

A black and white image appears, and a group of people are seen walking along a path.

"Play that again please," you ask, and this time you see it. The figure in the same clothes, walking along a street. Your eyes move to the time... after they turned into the wood. You've found the killer as they leave... and the footage goes on as your officers have tracked the figure to the local station, getting on a train.

"Well done, well done," you tell them, but they're laughing. "What is it?"

203

"You want well done? We lose all sight of the figure, but only after this..." and you watch as the figure gets off a train and disappears into a crowd.

"Where is that?"

"Sheffield," they say still laughing.

"And...?"

"Well, while we were taking a break from the footage, we looked this Path puzzle thing up on Amazon. And, well, turns out the designer lives in Sheffield..."

Turn to section 174.

⭑ 217

"You mean junk mail and that sort of thing?" you ask.

"Err... not exactly chief," the newsagent replies.

"Go on..."

"Well, err, it might be better to show you. I just sling the stuff out yunno, so I don't really know do I, if you know what I mean, but if you actually looked in the bin, right, you'd see, and..."

"Yes, of course, you wouldn't have said anything to me," and you nod.

"Phew, right yes, come with me."

He guides you round the back, and you come to a bin. Not one people put food or drink in, but the sort shredded paperwork was consigned to. The newsagent looks inside, pulls out a pile of papers and looks. "Yeah, right, here, look at this, three letters for Mr Forrest."

He hands them over to you. The first is simple enough, an advert for a food delivery company. But the second has the crest of a well-known credit card firm on it, and from inside you can see a lot of red text. Hadn't Mr Forrest said the book was selling well?

Mrs Forrest had binned this, she wasn't expecting to see it again... you open the letter, pull it out and discover that not only are the Forrests in a great deal of debt, they were also ignoring repayments requests...
"See what I mean..." says the newsagent.
Indeed you do. "Thanks very much," you tell him.

You gain keyword MAIL. Use this in headquarters to follow this lead up.

Return to headquarters by turning to section 75.

218

You will now be dropping into the homes of the Catan Cartel to speak to them.

For Baxter Hewitt, you may add five minutes and turn to section 18.
For Greg Helsh, you may add five minutes and turn to section 72.
For Caroline Krasinski, you may add five minutes and turn to section 121.
For Jay Weald you may add five minutes and turn to section 195.
Or return to section 46.

219

You follow up by asking, "Did you speak to Webb?"
Baxter replies "As before, I am going to clarify your definition with that."

With no hint of frustration you ask, "While you were reading his blog, and I presume his social media…"
"Yes."
"… did you exchange messages with each other. Online contact?"
"No, I did not talk to him, or exchange messages, I only read his work. I have no respect for the man but it's a fool who doesn't pay attention to his rivals."
"So you considered him a rival?" you ask innocently.
Baxter snorts. "No. As I said, the man was an idiot. Webb got so far and was nakedly trying to use other people to go the rest of the distance."
"People like you?" you ask.
"People who suffer fools. I have everything under control. I do not arrange meetings with puzzle groups and attempt to pump them for information while pretending I am cleverer than I am. That sort of thing leads to trouble."
"And you don't look for trouble?"
"No. Evidently Webb found it, and I suppose I should not be surprised. But the country is full of travellers."

Turn back to section 231 to continue.

220

There are ten uniformed officers, and an equal number of support staff, and they are in a line. This is difficult because they're also in a wood, and they are slowly making their way forward through the undergrowth, searching the earth for a body. Dealve said it had been killed recently, his spree was a recent one, and he did the barest necessary to cover the corpse, just a few branches thrown over… so it should be relatively easy to find if his map was accurate. Or if he was telling the truth. As the police search, aided by yourself and Robertson, all in plastic gloves, time passes, more and more until you become convinced there's no corpse here and this is just, as they say, a wild goose chase.

It gets to a point where you stand upright, feel your back having had enough, and decide, "Okay everyone, take a break." You turn to Robertson. "Would you agree we give up? There's nothing where he said or anywhere near."

"I would concur."

"Okay folks, wrap it up, thanks for your time.

To search for body one, add five minutes and turn to section 178.

To tell the man to stop wasting police time, turn to section 292.

221

"What do you do for a living?" you ask Greg.

"I recently became self-employed and am a full-time app designer, coder, and reviewer."

"Full-time reviewer?"

"Yeah, yeah, I have a YouTube channel and I talk about other people's apps. Everything Wrong With This App it's called, and I give stuff a right bollocking."

"I see."

"Then you've got my own company, G-Man Games, I'm G-Man cos I'm, Greg yeah..."

"Yes."

"And we do some games, some other useful apps, hey look, can I show you one? Yeah," and he pulls his mobile phone out and presses a few buttons. "Those are me at the top, you ever seen any?"

You thank the SOCO officer, but they have something else to say.

"We found hairs on the jacket of the victim. Possibly transferred in the killing. They're not human, I mean we could still get DNA from them if needed, but they're fur from a cat."

To speak to Phyllis' husband, turn to section 7.
To search Phyllis' office, turn to section 235.
To move on with the investigation, turn to section 46.

223

There are few things crisper and whiter than the white coat Aashi Clarif always wears, although it's often removed as she's changed into the white coveralls the job requires. She's the head Scene of Crime Officer for your county, and you've arranged to meet her in her office which happens to be in the same expansive building someone ordered the budget spent on. You bring her a large mocha and she greets you with a warm handshake. If it wasn't for the coat, Clarif would have looked at home lecturing in history as a long tenured professor. Her hair has turned from black to grey, but her smile lights up the wrinkles of her face.

"I won't keep you in small talk," she begins, nodding thanks as she takes the coffee. "My team have been all over the woods and the items found. I will disappoint you straightaway: we have only found one set of fingerprints on the car, those of Webb who was driving. If the passenger touched anything, it's been wiped or there were gloves. No fibres either, which is simply unlucky. We've got a print of the footwear the killer was wearing, at least we presume it's the killer after we ruled out the footwear of the victim and the jogger, but sadly it's not an unusual brand. A Nike trainer.

The knife is interesting, but of no more help to you. An eight-inch blade, kitchen knife, but it's not new: someone's been using this, we presume in their home, for a while, it's been thoroughly cleaned before the murder, and there's no prints. Given the victim's blood over it, we again presume the killer wore gloves, but no sign of them. The knife bent near the hilt under the violence of the assault. As for the victim, we did find some unusual hairs on the victims hoodie, but they're not human, so no DNA. In fact no DNA at all. The killer was extremely violent but planned this."

You nod as Clarif finishes. Sometimes, a killer leaves their complete handprint in the blood. Other times, it's like chasing a ghost.

You thank Clarif, leave her to drink her coffee and return to your office. Go to section 100.

Go to section 100.

⋆ 224

"...how would you sum Glen up?"

"He's just a big guy who wears his heart on his... actually Glen's got a violent streak. I don't want to bad-mouth the guy, and I know saying he threw out a guy who later got murdered doesn't paint him in a good light, but in for a penny: I would hate to live with Greg. It would be murder. He'd have me terrified he was going to go off. He seems to like all of the Cartel and put up with us, but I know the rest of the world isn't so lucky. It's his kids I feel for, although... I've never been interested in kids myself. I... wish to stop this line of questioning there."

"How about Caroline and Baxter?"

"Baxter's harmless, in fact that princess of a cat of his is probably more deadly with her birds, and mice, and whatever else cats get up to. As for Caroline, aren't most killers men? Be a good alibi wouldn't it, a female serial killer no one suspects because of millennia of accumulated misogyny."

"Good idea for a puzzle..." you tell Jay. "You can have that one for free." He doesn't laugh.

Turn back to section 280.

✦ 225

This is incorrect. Turn to section 300.

226

"No thanks," you say turning down Hewitt's offer, "I would prefer it if an officer does it instead. DC Robertson?" you finish speaking loudly, and Robertson comes over from keeping the rest of the Cartel in good order. "Can you please contact..."

"... Hewitt's Chemist."

"... Hewitt's Chemist and get their CCTV please."

"Sure thing."

You watch as Robertson uses her phone to google the details of Hewitt's Chemist, ring them and speak. You turn back to the man himself to ask more questions but notice out of the corner of your eye Robertson has pulled a face. You turn once more, unable to lip read the conversation, fascinated to know what's got such a reaction from such a theoretically simple task. Hewitt has turned too, so you study his face and find it impassive, waiting, no clue as to whether he knows what's being discussed. The phone call seems to get more heated, before Robertson clicks the phone off and comes over waving it around in her hand.

"A problem, Inspector."

"Go on Constable?" you ask, leaning forward in genuine excitement at what this new wrinkle will be.

"The CCTV at the chemist isn't working.

Turn to section 8.

• 227

In the end, you don't go to where the red Ford was stopped, because uniform and their squad car managed to pull her over on a busy road, so they then directed her to a side street, with one of the officers staying in her car to make sure. They pulled up in a road with little movement through, and Robertson squeezes her car in and as you get out you can see the Ford, the driver's door open, and the woman sat sideways in it with her legs coming out of the car. It is definitely Winnie Forrest.

"Hello there," you say as you go over, and you have a quick word with the uniformed officers, asking them to stay for a moment in case they were needed. You don't know what's going on, and it's entirely possible Winnie needs to be supported.

"We did a breath test on her," the officer says, "but that's come back clean. It's just the driving, endless erratic loops."

"Understood," you say, and you go over.

"Hello Mrs Forrest," you say introducing yourself. She looks down at the floor, ashamed of what's happening.

"What's going on here then?"

212

If you have the keyword Alpha, turn to section 104.
If you don't, turn to section 290.

❧ 228

You ask Greg, "How did he react?"

"Oh, he scarpered. Ran right off. Rest of the Cartel weren't happy, I reckon, cos I dunno if they found him any better, but they all agreed he'd been rude, yeah, he didn't like being shouted at."

"Do you not like rude people?" you ask innocently enough.

"Nah, why would I? Why should I? I got a life, and a mind, and I'm a human, and I don't have to take people talking shit to me, or starting trouble so yeah, if some little shit's gonna come into my group of friends and treat me like a servant or something, I'm gonna call that little shit out cos I'm a big shit and I will not fucking have it!" He has been getting louder and louder and finishes shouting and gesturing.

"But you'd never hurt Mr Webb? You didn't hurt Mr Webb?"

"Just his poxy fucking feelings. I'd not kill him, and I don't want you trying to fit me up neither. It's just a game for fuck's sake, you can't kill someone over a fucking game. It's not like the military or something."

"You've been in the military?"

"Nah, just an example, where you can kill someone."

"Do you not find it odd you take such exception to 'rude' people, but you've actually hit someone after an argument?"

Greg looks at you like he was about to leap over and try and tear your arms off, but he seems to have clung on to

213

something in him and he instead just replies, "anymore like that and I'll get my lawyer in."

Return to section 166 to continue questioning.

229

You open the book carefully, and find something very interesting... wait a minute, you're not supposed to be reading this section, there's no link to it in the book. Please don't read pages until you're sent to them, or you will spoil the mystery.

230

All around the fly-tipped area are footprints, but some are fresh and muddy and as you hoped, when you pass carefully through the gate on to the road, the prints continue a short way. You head down the road looking from side to side. There's hedgerows up to your waist, and beyond those fields which have been sowed with crops. It would be a nice, rural walk if you weren't trying to find where a potential suspect had run off to.
You come to a gate, and something catches your eye. It's not clean, it's been standing in all weathers for years, but as you kneel and look you notice fresh mud on the bars... someone's climbed over this recently. You and Robertson take a different approach, opening the gate – which is wide enough to cover a gap a tractor could drive through – and make sure to close it behind you. The country code isn't exactly in your hometown police training, but you still know it.

A trail leads away down the side of the field, where nothing had been sowed. Ignoring the sign which says, 'NOT A FOOTPATH', you continue down the trail as if it was.

Turn to section 254.

231

Baxter Hewitt sits opposite you, glowering. You watch as he runs his fingers through his short hair, as if it was once longer and has been shaved, and then takes his glasses from his shirt pocket and puts them on his nose, apparently purely so he can stare down them in contempt at you. You have clearly riled the man, and the questions must proceed in reaction to this.
"Would you like to stop for a drink?" you ask Hewitt to try and reset things.
"No, I would like to get this finished so I can return to my shop and keep the lights on, and then so I can get back to The Path, a puzzle I am far closer to solving than you obviously are with all this," and he waves his hands around him.

To ask, 'Did you know the victim?' turn to section 42.
To ask, 'Were you at the meeting?' turn to section 53.
To ask, 'Where were you the night of murder?' turn to section 22.
To ask, 'Was anyone angry at the victim?' turn to section 123.
To ask, 'Do you have any ideas about the murder?' turn to section 47.
To return to the Cartel, turn to section 212.

"Mr Gareth Hyax has been murdered," you tell Hewitt. "Did you know Mr Hyax at all?"

"No, I can confirm I did not know him."

"But had you heard of him?"

"I know you think I sit here all day and research every single thing about this case, but I assure you Inspector, I don't memorise every Tom, Dick or Harry who chose to write about the Path. Do I know him? Of him? No, that name is not in my memory. Have I, in the course of my writing, have come across his work and rejected it as irrelevant? Most probably, most probably."

"I see."

"Why don't you try and refresh my memory?"

"He edited Puzzle! magazine, which was releasing a special on The Path, to set up a future solution issue."

"Really? Well, doesn't jog my memory."

"Puzzle! magazine once ran an article on your father..."

"Yes, yes, I know Puzzle! magazine, but I couldn't have told you who edited now, or then, or if they were different."

To ask where they were at the time of Hyax's murder, turn to section 102.

To ask if they know anyone angry at Hyax, turn to section 36.

To ask if Hewitt has any ideas about the murder, turn to section 5.

To leave Hewitt, return to section 129.

233

You begin with, "Regarding the meeting between the Catan Cartel and Mr Webb..." but Krasinski interrupts you.

"Yes, that took place."

"Okay, thanks, we're certain of that but..."

"It was in this very room. We all sat along that table like we were interviewing him for a job, or Dragon's Den or something. Looking back it wasn't very friendly, but we did spend a while on musical chairs before Baxter decided to stick us all down one side. Webb didn't seem worried, he seemed like he'd put up with it in order to get information out of us."

"I see, thanks for the description. Why where you at the meeting?"

"I'm the most successful member of the Cartel," Krasinski said beaming.

"How does that translate into coming to the meeting?"

"Well I presumed I'd be the one he'd recognise, and expect to see, and I find it my responsibility to always be the face of the Cartel."

"So you've mentioned them on television?"

"More than a few times! I think we're famous, at least in puzzling circles, thanks to my winnings. I bet people give a sigh when they check winner's lists in their magazines and see me."

To ask about the others in the group, turn to section 284.
To ask more about The Path, turn to section 101.

▪ 234

"Did you have any later contact with Mr Webb, after the meeting?"

"I bet you're thinking, Jay wouldn't have had any, if his whole technique is to sit back and let others do the pressing, but let's be honest, I'd be remiss if I let anything pass me by, so I took his contact number. It's even in my phone, look," and he waves his phone at you. Webb's number is there, but there's no messages.

"He never contacted you?" you ask.

"I must have left such a terrible impression he didn't sniff round me. One wants to be regarded as clever, but one doesn't want to actually give away any answers, being considered the village idiot is a problem if Webb ever finds anything out. Or should I say had he found anyone out. Very difficult to get the tense right with these things, you must have a right nightmare with it."

"To be honest the tenses I use isn't a major concern."

"That's why you're a police officer and I'm a proofreader and editor."

"And a game designer too?"

Jay looks awkwardly at the floor and squirms in his seat.

Return to section 293 to ask more questions.

ᴗ 235

You head back towards Phyllis' office, and your car, but as you walk you can hear sirens, lots and lots of sirens, and you break into a run and come out into the back of the office buildings... which are on fire. A firefighter gestures for you to get back to safety, and you end up stood by your car watching the water hose through the windows of the office.

After a while, it's obvious the firefighters have gained control, and soon enough the flames have gone, and smoke is left to rise in plumes from burnt and wet wood.

A firefighter goes up to make sure no one was inside, following a report from one of the other offices that a staffer was missing, but they are soon found safe outside. In the aftermath, you're able to speak to that firefighter.

"You investigating this?" she says to you.

"Yes, I am. Why?"

"Well, it's arson, definitely arson, and I say this cos in the psycho's office someone's piled all the paper files and the computers up in the middle and set the whole thing to burn, that's what caused it.

You thank her for the information.

To speak to Phyllis' receptionist, turn to section 50.
↓ To check the CCTV footage, turn to section 263.

236

You conclude the single set of footprints leading away from the clearing are those of the killer, so taking care not to step on them you tail the trail through the wood. If you could put the murder aside, the way the morning light filters through the canopy would be a pleasant sight, reminding you of the need to spend less time in the office and more out... then the path takes a turn, and you find a ford. Across the path a stream runs, something that could easily be walked across, and is every day, but which still delights a part of you.

Then you see the knife.

Glinting up from the stream, but immersed in it, is a carving knife. You step cautiously over and see not just blood on the implement – an awful lot of blood – but something else in the stream next to it. You pull out rubber gloves, don them, and then pick up a wallet, which you flip open to find a driving licence belonging to

Harold Webb, and a photo of the man who lay dead behind you. Turning your attention back to the knife, you see the point has bent under the pressure of the assault, but the knife looks like something you could buy in any supermarket. Has the killer tried to wash evidence off by dumping the knife and wallet here? You don't know, but you send Stewart to get forensics as you guard the scene. You feel certain this is the murder weapon...

After a short while the forensics technicians secure the site and you're able to head back to headquarters to begin your investigation and await their report.

It's time to return to headquarters and set up, turn to section 100.

It's time to return to headquarters and set up, turn to section 100.

237

You sit down at your desk and prepare a new briefing sheet which claims to contain new information gathered by your team back home, and how it reflects on the Sheffield area. You then alter this sheet in certain key places, so everyone it's given to has a different piece of key information, and then you hand everyone their sheets. It's now just a matter of checking in on the Local Mirror website every now and again to see if their live rolling coverage of the event has been updated.

Luckily for your hopes of find the mole, Morton is the sort of man who loves a huge red text saying 'live' and regular posts with his name on them, aka making the people of Sheffield hang on his every word. In fact you make a small bet with yourself on how long it's going to take your mole to give Morton the 'fact' and for it to appear. Robertson has no idea this is happening, because in all honesty you can't trust anyone here, you've known them for simply a few days, but you feel bad about not including her in the skullduggery / detective work.

Turn to section 281.

⚡ 238

"What can you tell me about the puzzle?" you ask Jay.
"Ah," and he turns and looks behind him at the Cartel as if he's about to be a naughty child.
"What's wrong?" you ask.
"They won't like me saying this..."
"Go on."
"I'm a game designer, and I am approaching The Path with one eye on how it's constructed and all that minutiae of construction I won't bore you with. What I can say, is that..." and he leans forward and whispers, "it's not that good. Hard, as a puzzle yes, but not that good."
You ask, "Can you give us an example?"
"Just a basic one, but you've got to take pride in your work, and travellers can quickly work out quite a few images in The Path are purchased from photo libraries. Gato hasn't even sourced his own original pieces!"
"That's a problem?"
"Yes, for a designer like me, who wants to be perfect and legendary, the fact it's got stock material is a big turn off. I'd still back it on Kickstarter, but I wouldn't have my hopes high. I don't know if the others have the same problem, we've never been openly critical of the work to each other, in 'public' as it were."

To ask Jay what the puzzle means to him, turn to section 45.

To ask Jay what he thinks of the others in the group, turn to section 265.

239

Dear Mr Gato Blanc,

We have been conversing for a while, but you have proved frustrating beyond ends. You are an arrogant know it all who lords over us travellers, and now has come the time to put the façade behind us. The Path is your mirage, but behind it lies a puzzle. I want the answer to that puzzle, as you have made it deliberately impossible to be solved. Gato Blanco is a façade, because I know you are Reginald Forest, and this anonymous letter is a façade, because you will not know who I am until you have made true your falsehood and told me the answer. I say answer, but answer demands a question and you have posed no question. The Path is a fake. I have poured my life into it Forest, and it is impossible, by your hand, to continue to sell books. You will tell me the answer Mr Forest, or I will hurt you until you do. Do you understand? I can ruin you mentally, I can ruin you physically. Or you can be honest for the first time in your life and tell me where the climax of The Path lies.

Yours, X.

Return to section 120.

240

Forest!

I have not heard from you about my last letter. This is a mistake, on your part, because you are receiving these letters in the post, and you know what that means... it means I know where you live. I must do, if I am sending you letters! Surely you are not stupid enough to not realise I could visit your house, right now, this second, and force you to tell me where you put the climax of The Path? A Path, need I repeat, which you made deliberately false and impossible for me to follow. If there was a right answer, I would have found it. If there was a real puzzle here, I would have completed it, I would be rich. But you... you lied, and you teased, and you made me devote hours to this, hours, which I will not get back, but which will be worth it when you tell me, even if I have to beat it out of you. Reply to me, Forest, or I will come for you like a god of vengeance.

X.

You turn the letter over and back. There is no return address, phone number, meeting place or any way at all for Forrest to reply, should he have wanted to.

Return to section 120.

⋆ 241

Forest, I may not need you. You may have been talking to other people and not me, which is a mistake for you all. I have a meeting, with a man who claims he knows where the climax of The Path is. Not that he's solved it all, because that would be impossible, but he's gone outside the book and worked it out... and I have a meeting with him. I'm going to kill him Forest, partly because I can't risk someone else finding the money when I have placed so much of myself into the game. But I'm also doing it to show you what will happen if you don't tell me. The clock is ticking Forest, I will come and find you, and I will kill again, and next time it may well be you. Tell me, tell me, confess all your sins of your impossible task and maybe then you can live a happy and content life free of your crime. If you tell me, I won't blab it was all fake. We can carry on. Tell me you fucking snake. Tick tock, tick tock.

X, or 'the last person you will ever see'.

Return to section 120.

242

"In here!" Winnie half screams. All four of you rush in, and you find Winnie in the kitchen. She is stood in one corner, forcing herself into the wall and looks at you with desperation.
"When I got home, the door was open, we never leave the door open, we don't have a cat, but hanging open, and when I came in here, I see all the mugs smashed, the plates on the floor," and she's right, there is debris everywhere, "and then I saw that..." She points.
Your eyes follow and you see a plastic packet which used to contain four kitchen knives just purchased from a supermarket. The main, and largest, knife is missing.
"The killer has my husband!" Winnie screams. You agree with her.

This is it, Detective. By now you should have enough information to know who the killer is. At your command police will rush round to arrest them and save Reginald Forrest before he too is killed. Who will you choose?

To arrest Caroline Krasinski, turn to section 30.
To arrest Jay Weald, turn to section 74.
* To arrest Baxter Hewitt, turn to section 283.
To arrest Greg Weald, turn to section 141.
To arrest Winnie Forrest, turn to section 211.

243

"Yeah, I guess I can tell you. I was at home working, programming app work."
You note this down and reply, "To be honest Greg, I'm not sure why that was such a secret."
"Ah, right, well I was having self-employed coffee, if you know what I mean."
You look at Robertson, who shrugs, so are forced to ask "I don't know what that is..."
"Alcohol. I got very blitzed that night and did most of my work drunk. Thing is I know how to present a professional image where my apps are and admitting you did most of it wankered isn't the way."
"Do you normally drink a lot?"
"Well, no more than the next guy. But I wasn't watching football I was coding."
"Sounds difficult to be honest," you tell him. "Do you have anyone who can corroborate that?"
"No. I was at home on the bevvies with my laptop. I guess you could look at my laptop and note the time stamps of everything to show I was using it then."
"You would allow our team to look at it?" you ask.
"Yeah, sure thing, I've nothing to hide, like."
"Perfect."

You receive the codeword LAPTOP.

Turn back to section 177 to continue questioning.

244

"Where were you at the time of the second murder?"
"Second? So you reckon they are connected? Well, it's a problem, cos I was at home here during that time, having a few beers and playing on the old PlayStation. Not puzzle games, shooting my way through the German army if you know what I mean."
"I see," and you turn to the video recorder he has on his TV stand. The timer on it is wrong and flickering. "Why is that doing that?"
"Oh, it does that after a power cut. Dunno why I keep the stupid thing except you can get massive bargains off the Facebook marketplace. I got the entire series of X-Files and Babylon 5 for free off one guy."
"And, given the time on that video recorder, which started from 00:00 when the power came back on, what time was it off?"
Greg looks at the flashing time, looks back at you, and realises the power must have been off when Hyax was murdered, which meant his alibi was shot to bits.
"If we go on any more about times I'll need my lawyer," he replies.

To ask, 'Did you know Gareth Hyax?' turn to section 159.
To ask if they know anyone angry at Hyax, turn to section 269.
To ask if Helsh has any ideas about the murder, turn to section 127.

226

To leave Helsh, return to section 129.

245

You take a deep breath. This is one of the hardest parts of the job, but one of the most necessary, so you walk slowly up the path to the house of Mr Webb's parents, who live in a detached house on the outskirts of the town. Everything is neat and ordered in the garden, and you tap lightly on the door, which is opened shortly after by a young woman in a suit, someone you know well. Trained in grief counselling, she's the first line of support you offer a family who, in this case, rang in this morning to report that their son wasn't answering his phone and hadn't come home all night, so to them was missing. Sadly, unlike most similar cases where someone just stayed out all night, Webb junior really wasn't coming home.

"Hello there," you say softly, and a red-eyed mother directs you to sit on a wooden chair that's been brought over.

A pale-faced father nods at you and says, "Suppose you've got questions."

"When was the last time you heard from Harold?"

"We speak to him several times a day. Well, he speaks to us," the mum replies, "recently he just rings us, babbles excitedly and has to go. It's nice he's been in contact but... his head's just full of that book. The Path."

"The Path?" you ask.

"The puzzle book. Then when he didn't call at all yesterday, and we went and his car was gone, and it was 3:00 am and we... we rang you. The police. You. But... it was too late?"

227

"Sadly we believe your son died yesterday evening. Do you know of anyone who'd have reason to hurt your son?"

"No, none at all," the dad said taking over. "He ran a website... he was a blogger. Unemployed to me, but he said he blogged all the time about his hobby, which was puzzles. Said he'd made a life on the website. Didn't think puzzles could kill someone."

"The money," the mum said sadly. "Someone wanted the money he was going to win."

"But you've no names or people he's mentioned?"

"No. It was all his work. He never connected anyone else. He had a few friends, but he was drifting away from them..." the mother's voice breaks. You sense it is time to leave things to your support officer.

Return to headquarters and turn to section 100.

246

"Did you know Mrs Phyllis Wright?" you ask Greg, and his face twitches.

"Mrs?" he replies.

"She was a psychiatrist..."

"Nah mate, never heard of her."

You follow up with, "You sure about that?"

He turns and points the wooden spoon he's holding at you. "I don't want you to disrespect me Inspector. If you know something, and you're getting at something, just tell me. Rude to stand there and try to fool me."

"Well, putting the whole asking questions part of policing aside then Mr Helsh, I know you had cause to visit Phyllis Wright for her professional services, and now she's dead.

228

Are you prepared to tell me why you went, how often, etc?"
"You probably find this easy to understand, I went for anger management. Since my arrest, weekly, try and calm me down. Do you reckon it's done any good?

To ask what they were doing at the time of the murder / arson, turn to section 24.
To ask if they knew any connection between Phyllis and The Path, turn to section 97.
To ask if they have any further ideas on the case, turn to section 273.
Or return to section 218.

247

"Do you know if anyone was angry at Mr Webb?" you ask Krasinski.
She makes a haughty laugh and says firmly, "Yes!"
"Who?"
"Well someone who killed him!"
You don't laugh, just nod and continue, "But in your dealings with him, was anyone angry at him?"
"I don't know of anyone I'd say angry... I mean the travellers are all a fairly highly strung bunch and there's plenty of heated discussions about minute detail, and that's one benefit of being by yourself on quiz shows, there's ultimately no one to tell you off, just you and millions of people if you check Twitter. I don't check Twitter."
"If we could stick to the investigation?"
"Yes, we all should. Well there's lots of angry people on The Path, but it's all jealousy. I don't think anyone would ever threaten anyone. I mean he did end up in a shouting

match when he was here, but no harm came from it, just two men getting their dicks bruised."

"Oh?"

"Yes, Glen got very riled up by his tone and ended up shouting at him, before he, err, Glen stormed off. Webb left shortly after, and I doubt he and Glen have spoken much since."

Turn to section 134.

248

"Miss Krasinski, did you know Mr G. Hyax?"

"No, but as I'm sure you're already aware, I nearly did."

"Go on?"

"Hyax is, was, the editor of Puzzle! He mentioned recently he had nearly finished The Path, and I, being somewhat naïve, wrote to him in his capacity as editor and journalist to ask if he could help me. I didn't put it quite as blatantly as that, but I did do just that. I was fully prepared to engage with him and have a chat, a discussion, a student teacher back and forth, but he never even replied to me. I'd like to think he was murdered before he could respond, but I assume what actually happened was he didn't think I was worth the time. Maybe he had solved The Path. Maybe he had. Wouldn't need the likes of me. But only you would know that I presume?"

"I am happy to confirm the police don't know the answer to The Path."

To ask where they were at the time of Hyax's murder, turn to section 65.

To ask if they know anyone angry at Hyax, turn to section 208.

To ask if Caroline has any ideas about the murder, turn to section 48.

To leave Caroline, return to section 129.

249

It's a warm day, and there's a gentle breeze to keep it cool. Thanks to the way the land rises and falls, you and Robertson are able to perch yourself in an old barn that overlooks a sloping field, and she's brought a cool box with cold drinks which is the kind of planning you can get behind. You've been sat there lightly chatting when you hear a car approaching. You make sure you're hidden and watch as the car stops on the lane, and a man steps out. He puts on a pair of green wellies, gets a small spade from the boot and makes his way across a broken patch of crops until he comes to the site he's been digging on earlier. You give a nod to Robertson, and she heads off to secure the car as you calmly and slowly work your way through the field towards him. The man hasn't noticed you because he's busy checking and re-checking his location, and he's just picking up the spade to dig again when you come up right behind him and say, "Excuse me sir, can you explain what you're doing?"

In the shock he screams and drops the spade but allows you to question him.

Turn to section 180.

You arrange to speak to all the Catan Cartel for a second time, this time you will be visiting them at their homes.

- For Baxter Hewitt you may add five minutes and turn to section 115.
- For Greg Helsh you may add five minutes and turn to section 20.

For Caroline Krasinski you may add five minutes and turn to section 198.

For Jay Weald you may add five minutes and turn to section 253.

Or return to section 129.

251

Caroline Krasinski looks at you as if she's having second thoughts about this whole process, and especially about your involvement in it. First, she looks at the floor, as if counting the strands of carpet, then she turns, notably makes eye contact with Robertson and raises an eyebrow, the universal language for 'is this person okay or some sort of nutter?' You can't see what expression Robertson pulls, but it makes Krasinski a little happier and she turns back to you. Evidently, you've not made a good impression on your new colleagues in Sheffield. You almost miss DC Stewart, who quietly put up with all of your eccentricities. Okay, not exactly quietly.

"Okay, I'm ready for more questions or can I go now?" Krasinski says, but the keenness she had earlier is gone.

"More or shall I go?"

That's up to you.

To ask, 'Did you know the victim?' turn to section 151.

To ask, 'Were you at the meeting?' turn to section 196.

To ask, 'Where were you the night of the murder?' turn to section 44.

To ask, 'Was anyone angry at the first victim?' turn to section 247.

To ask, 'Do you have any ideas about the murder?' turn to section 96.

To return to the Cartel, turn to section 212.

252

"I have to ask," you begin, "because I have absolutely no idea what you mean, so what's the 'Murder Wall'?"

Jay starts laughing, which isn't always a good sign. "Oh, I'm so sorry, I'm used to everyone knowing, they hear me talk about it all the time, in fact I'm sure they're all fed up and too polite to tell me to stop. You're probably the first people I've come into contact with in ages, besides Webb, that I haven't bored to death," and he finishes still laughing.

You nod, lean forward and say, "Yes, but what is it?"

"It's my game!" You and Robertson exhale slightly.

"I've played a lot of games, solved a lot of puzzles, but what I really want to do is make my own... and I am, in the form of Murder Wall. Now, unless you get me a lawyer I don't want to go into the mechanics because the details are secret ahead of finishing it and launching a Kickstarter, but yeah, it's my game. There's a murder, you solve a murder. Several."

"If it's secret, how have you bored people with it?" you ask.

"I might have told them the same thing over and over..."

Return to section 280.

253

You arrive at Jay's terraced house and knock on the front door... however you have to wait a while and then knock again, louder. This time there's the sound of stumbling feet and the door opens to Jay looking shocked. "Oh sorry Inspector, I lost track of the time, and I had my headphones in. Thin walls you see."
He turns and leads you down a corridor and into his lounge, and you stop so suddenly Robertson bangs into the back of you.
"Wow," you say in genuine surprise at what's in front of you. "The Murder Wall game has a real murder wall."
Across one entire wall in the lounge, the side with a boarded up fireplace, are maps, photographs, printouts, an entire amateur investigation's worth of whiteboarding, which you've presumed is for the much mentioned game. At least, you hopes it's for the game and Jay isn't five bodies deep into some unknown serial killer.
"Yes, yes, it is. My inspiration, and my working board. Everything starts here and then gets transformed into the game. People will be building their own replica of this at home."
He sounds confidant.

To ask, 'Did you know Gareth Hyax?' turn to section 259.
To ask where they were at the time of Hyax's murder, turn to section 107.
To ask if they know anyone angry at Hyax, turn to section 54.

To ask if Jay has any ideas about the murder, turn to section 144.

To leave Jay, return to section 129.

• 254

While you don't know for sure, you feel the crops are growing well, and in this field they're up above your waist. You continue down the trail and come to another gate: wide, worn, clear signs of muddy boots vaulting up over it. But what's that over there?

You open the gate and leave it for Robertson, who's behind you, and jog over to a patch of muddy earth by the side of the road. There's fresh tyre tracks in it, as if the person who burned the clothes had travelled over the fields back to their car and used it to drive away. Which is unfortunate, because that would be where the trail ended unless you could get any useful information to double check a car you later found, like the soil type.

"Inspector!" Robertson says behind you, and you turn to find her waving excitedly. You jog back, and see she's already slipped a rubber glove on one hand and leans down to pick something off the ground.

"What is it?" you ask.

"Looks like something could have fallen out of a pocket as they climbed the gate, it's a receipt... with a name on it. But it's fresh, on top of the mud, only very recent.

"Useful, but a long shot."

"Oh no Inspector," and Robertson winks, "I know the name. I know who this is, and it's no long shot at all."

Turn to section 111.

"Where were you yesterday at the time of the murder and arson?" you ask Hewitt.

"I was here. At home. I appreciate that's in no way a testable alibi, but I was here, in comfort, with Coco. Wasn't I Coco, tell the police I was here, yes?" The cat meows, although it's not clear if this is a yes or no. "See, she backs me up, I was here." You get the weird feeling Baxter is being serious about it confirming the alibi.

"Sadly animal testimony is not recognised in court," you say. "If so, Diddles the cat might have been able to tell the world who Jack the Ripper was. But that was a different time and case."

"Inspector, have you gone quite mad?"

You don't tell him that's rich coming from him.

"Maybe your neighbours or anyone saw you?" you offer.

Baxter sighs, "I have no alibi. The world does not diarise me all the time."

To ask if he knew Phyllis Wright, turn to section 213.
To ask if they knew any connection between Phyllis and The Path, turn to section 125.
To ask if they have any further ideas on the case, turn to section 63.
To move on, return to section 218.

"You seem convinced he wasn't killed for the puzzle?"

"Ah, I'm convinced no one here killed him. Someone down there might have, there's travellers all over the place. But if I didn't kill him, and I'm stressing this right now," he points at you, "if I didn't kill him, then no one in the Cartel did."

"What makes you so sure?"

"They're all so soft. Kras is a woman, so she's out, Baxter's whatever kind of man has more interest in his fucking cat than people, and Jay's just timid. None of them have the balls to fucking kill a guy. So, if it's Path people you'll have to find who else Webb was talking too, cos it's no one here."

You deliberately look down to make some notes, then look back up, "But isn't that the best way to be? Not someone who'd kill?"

"Nah mate, loads of fuckers in this world who need a telling off. Social media lets people get away with shit all the time, cos no one would say that stuff to my face. People are soft, we've lost the art of backing up the bollocks you're saying with some presence. I reckon I should stop talking there."

Turn back to section 177.

⟩ 257

This is incorrect. Turn to section 300.

⟩ 258

"What can you tell me about The Path?" you ask Hewitt. He answers, "I assume you don't want a complete page-by-page breakdown of the solution so far discovered, because I want protest to a lawyer about sharing that confidential information."

You smile politely back as him. "No, just in general."

"These puzzle books come out every so often, none of them ever became as popular as Masquerade who I think you'll find is the daddy. But The Path resonated with a lot of people I believe, certainly a hundred thousand pound prize will do that, and as you no doubt know the author is local, and perhaps the solution is too... the Cartel members seized on it quickly. We're trendsetters. A lot of almost as dedicated people are following in our footsteps, and I know I mustn't slip up or people will overtake me."

"It matters then, that the author is local?"

"Gato Blanc being in the same city... yes, I think it does, although I couldn't tell you why. I would have to think a lot more about that, oh yes, I would. I mean I know he's got a real name too, of course, don't put me down as ignorant.

Turn to section 287.

259

You ask Jay, "Have you ever heard of Gareth Hyax before?"

"Oh yes, I've heard of him all right."

"That's an interesting tone to your voice, how have you heard of him?"

"Well it'd be hard not to have heard of him after Greg rang me to tell me he'd seen this post where the person, victim, editor called Hyax was nearly at the Panda!"

"Greg rang you?"

"Yep."

"Did he ring anyone else?"

"I don't know. He rings me a lot to show off news he's found, I think he likes being thought of as contributing

238

given he's gone downhill recently since his wife left. I feel like I'm the one Greg speaks to most of the Cartel. But yeah, he called, and I had a good snoop round the web. No Wikipedia page, but a biography on the Puzzle! website. Oddly, after hearing I stuck in a year's subscription to the magazine because it seemed good. I guess that's over with now!"

To ask where they were at the time of Hyax's murder, turn to section 107.
To ask if they know anyone angry at Hyax, turn to section 54.
To ask if Jay has any ideas about the murder, turn to section 144.
To leave Jay, return to section 129.

260

"A couple of times just now you've alluded to something happening in your life. Something that might be good or bad because you went self-employed seemingly at the same time."
"Ah, nah, some shit happened, yeah, and... well, I lost my job and I set myself up doing my thing and yeah, the income is less but I'm my own boss now and... the real boss left. The real boss left me."
"Who's that?"
Greg looks genuinely upset as he says, "My wife. She left me over it all, over what happened. Dunno why she turned on me, you're through thick and thin, married couples, yeah, and she left me to rot, the bi... I'd take her back, but she just walked out on me, took the kids, got some lawyers and started to divorce me. Wants the house. Tell you what I could do with winning The Path to

pay her off, really could. The apps don't make much money, but she'd only take it anyway. Stupid... yeah, she ruined my life. For no reason. A man has a few problems, and a marriage ends. Fucking hell. What a state. And I was the only one of the Cartel to be fucking married!"
"My condolences," you add, not knowing if that's the right word at all.

Turn back to section 177.

Turn back to section 177.

⤬ 261 ⤬

You tap your phone off and move down the yard area, to find the large wooden fence has a gate in it. There's a heavy bolt to keep it closed, but that bolt is on your side and currently open, so the gate just smoothly swings towards you at a touch. Beyond is a thick woodland, and a path leading away into it. The route isn't well-travelled, but there are relatively fresh foot marks, so you head along into the wood. It's a straightforward journey initially as there's just one trail and it leads ahead, with little chance for anyone to have gone off the path. You move as quietly as you can to aid in listening, but you can't hear anything untoward, not a struggle nor a human moving. Just birds fluttering between higher branches and a crow cawing.
Finally you come to a fork in the path. There's three routes converging, the one you're on and two others. One has multiple footprints and goes to the left. Another has one set of footprints, slower boot prints, and goes to the right. Which will you follow?

To go left, turn to section 112.
To go right, turn to section 57.

240

You knock on a white wooden door that's to the left of Webb's flat when you're facing it... and wait. Nothing happens, but you can hear a radio on inside and the sound of a Radio 2 DJ yapping, so you knock again but much louder.

"Hang on!" someone shouts annoyed from inside, and a few moments later the door is yanked open. Pipe smoke comes curling out at you, followed by a bearded older man.

"Hello sir, I was hoping..." you only get to begin.

"You got my parcel?"

"No sir."

"Oh, why don't you have my parcel?"

"I'm not...."

"No cold callers! No cold callers, none of your church stuff and none of your sales stuff."

"Sir, I am a detective with the local police force."

"I don't have a TV licence; I don't agree with it."

"I'd just like to ask you a few questions about your neighbour."

"Oh. Right. Sorry. Yeah. Go on."

"Has Mr Webb lived next door long?"

"That his name, is it? Mr Webb?"

"You didn't know his name?"

"Nah, didn't know the guy at all."

"Did you see any people here last night? Going into or coming from his flat?"

"Nah, I'm drunk in the evenings watching the soaps."

"Okay, thank you for your time."

You step back and he shuts the door. Not everyone is in a position to help the police...

To speak to the neighbour opposite, turn to section 291.

↪ 263

As you've been watching the fire you've noticed a CCTV camera fixed high up on to the wall. It should have sent a clear image of everyone entering and leaving these shops and offices, so all you need to do is give the provider a call and get the image sent over to you... and yet something is nagging you in the back of your mind. So, with the fire put out and dampening going on, you walk over to the parade of shops and see the camera has a cable going out the back, fixed to the wall and turning the corner. You move round to the back of the shops like you did before and go to where the cable comes round... and there you see it. Someone has climbed on to one of the yellow dumpsters and cut the cable to the camera. Whether it provided data or power, the camera has been neutralised. There's no image of the killer or Mrs Wright leaving. However, you have to make sure, so you place the call... only for them to confirm it. This avenue is no help.

To speak to Phyllis' husband, turn to section 7.
To wait and speak to the scene of crime team about their findings, turn to section 222.
To move on the investigation, turn to section 46.

264

"And yet, Mr Webb was invited to speak at the Cartel? Did everyone share your opinion of him?"

Krasinski laughs, "No, people disliked even the hustle. I know it sounds odd for all four of us to sit here and slag off a man who we invited along, but I know none of us wanted to miss the chance to pick his brains. Why miss a chance to question him, if we could use that by letting him to try and question us."

"Try?"

"Oh, he was as bad at questioning as you are, and none of us had any plan to share real information, or even do a fair exchange. We'd brought him in for one-way traffic, and let me tell you, that was a real disappointment. Same as this too. We all soon knew this was a waste of time. At least I did. The others might have slightly different views, but they didn't admit to any afterwards. We all talk a lot, the Cartel, and we did have a little laugh about Webb behind his back... oh that makes me feel bad now. It's hard to believe he's actually dead and gone."

Turn to section 145 to continue the questioning.

⟨ 265

"What are your views on the others in the Cartel?"

Jay smiles and replies, "Well that's a marvellously open question isn't it. What are my views on them... I'm not going to tell you they're nice people. I'm not convinced any of us are nice people!" He almost cackles. "What I can tell you is we're all trying to outdo each other. We all come to the meetings, and we say nice things, but really, we're showing off, and trying to one-up, and the tension near the end of a game, or the completion of a puzzle challenge is so high. We all like friendly enemies, people who you desperately want to beat but stay friends with because no one else would understand the achievement.

Yes, I'd say that all right. Even Greg, he knows he needs us, so we all stumble on us four."

"There's never been anyone else?"

"Yes, over the years a few have come for a while, but they all leave soon enough. I suspect we're just all intense wankers, if I can say that to a police officer."

You reply, "I've heard it a lot before."

To ask Jay if he's ever tested his work on the Cartel, turn to section 172.

To ask Jay about the puzzle, turn to section 238.

Otherwise turn back to section 280.

266

This is incorrect. Turn to section 300.

267

A man walks over to where you've set up but looks in a passing mirror before he gets to you, pauses, pulls off some long cat hairs from his shirt, then comes over and sits. He's six foot tall, of average build, and has shortly cropped hair that was once either fair or ginger and is now mostly grey. He wears a business shirt and trousers but no jacket, although you notice there's a white coat laid with his bag back over with the rest of the Cartel. His eyes are a steely blue, and his face is raw and recently shaved.

"Hello there," you say and introduce yourself.

"I'm Baxter Hewitt," he says to return the favour, and he peers over at the notes you're taking in your ever-present book. "I suppose you want to add that I'm thirty-seven, unmarried, and a fully qualified pharmacist who owns my own shop." He seems very keen for you to add that point. "And yes, I am that Hewitt." He stops and looks at you as if realisation is going to hit you.

"That Hewitt?" you ask.

He instantly looks annoyed, and at you like you're a fool. "Hewitt, I am Baxter Hewitt, son of Alfred Hewitt, the Times crossword setter and puzzle master. I assumed you were involved in a case involving The Path because you knew something about the world of puzzles."

"Your father was famous?"

"My father was royalty," and he could have been hissing.

"And you're..."

"A successful pharmacist."

* To ask, 'Did you know victim?' turn to section 64.
* To ask, 'Were you at the meeting?' turn to section 209.
* To ask, 'Where were you the night of the murder?' turn to section 66.
* To ask, 'Was anyone angry at the first victim?' turn to section 168.
* To ask, 'Do you have any ideas about the murder?' turn to section 99.
* To ask more about his father, turn to section 201.

To return to the Cartel, turn to section 212.

268

"Mr Webb was working on puzzle book, The Path, and that's what he was invited to the Cartel to speak about, wasn't it?"

"Yeah, that's right."

"What can you tell me about The Path?"

"I consider myself expert on puzzle books, but I'm late to the party."

"How do you mean?"

"Well, you heard of Masquerade, yeah?"

"Yes."

"So if I gave you a copy of Masquerade, and you sat down and solved it, and didn't look anything up on the web or owt, you'd say you solved it, even though it's been like forty years."

"Seems fair to me," you tell him.

"Well then, I've solved Masquerade then, and lots of other puzzle books. I mean Escape Rooms are expensive, travel and all that, so I do other puzzles and when I heard The Path was coming out, I did my research, put my hours in, did some of the others."

"That makes sense. Did anyone else in the group do that?"

"Baxter did, he's done as much as possible to prepare, while Kras just did her usual thing of rocking up to it and hoping she wins. Nah, I'm doing her down, she spends a lot of time cramming her head with facts for the gameshows."

Turn to section 192.

269

You ask Greg, "Do you know anyone angry at the victims?"

"Nah chief, nah, it wouldn't be anger would it. What do we know about Webb? Rude bastard, but said he was near the answer. What you told me about Hyax? Maybe he was rude too, but he bragged too. Someone killed two people who said they were near the Panda... so that tells me we got someone killing their competition. Imagine if Baxter posted up he was a day away from the solution, someone would chop his fucking head off, right? Well it's not anger, we all got the pull in us, the need to stop them. That's your motive, that's your motive right there."

"And do you know anyone like that?" you ask.

"Yeah chief, all of us. All of us on the Path are like that. It gets into you. It's magnetic. I mean, I wouldn't kill a guy on purpose, but I can see why someone would.

To ask, 'Did you know Gareth Hyax?' turn to section 159.

To ask where they were at the time of Hyax's murder, turn to section 244.

To ask if Helsh has any ideas about the murder, turn to section 127.

To leave Helsh, return to section 129.

✒ 270

You ask Krasinski, "You don't consider a shouting match a sign of anger?"

"Well, err..." and she squirms in her seat not wanting to answer. She's clearly trying not to give you something specific.

"Please," you ask sincerely, "any information could help. We don't know if this killer will strike again." Which, sadly, was very true, especially if this was all about solving The Path.

"Okay, the thing is Glen does have a violent streak. He shouts, he swears, he bangs tables, he's been asked to leave from events over the years for getting in the face of people, yeah, that's out there but... to us he's Glen."

You follow up with, "He has ever hurt anyone physically?"

"No. No. I mean not that I know of, I don't know everything about him, if you see what I mean. I wouldn't feel threatened in his company."

"But has he ever shouted at you?"

"Err..." she thinks, taking this seriously, the truth of the situation becoming apparent, "no, no, I suppose he hasn't. I guess if he had screamed in my face, I wouldn't feel okay around him. But he's always been a gentleman to me."

Turn to 153 to continue questioning.

☞ 271

As you step out of the shop, Robertson pulls out her phone and begins to call to see what CCTV is operating on the pavements in this area. While she does this you walk down the narrow street and stick your head in the next shop, which is on the other side of the road.

"Excuse me," you ask the florist inside, "but did you see a man run past here yesterday?"

"Yeah, yeah I did, went that way," and she points to further down the road. So that means...

You follow the street down, looking for where the runaway might have gone. It's long, narrow, and has no more shop units in it, just brick walls with fading white paint. When you get to the end there's a gate, which is hanging open and loose, and it goes into a narrow footpath which passes the back of a pub. There's more than the usual amount of pub rubbish piled up here, and you can't see anyone to ask so you start to carefully have a look about.

There, behind a pile of pallets, shoved in, is a dull coloured hoodie, a baseball cap, and an actual adult-sized wig. There's little chance of two people dumping this material, and you are fascinated to find the hoodie and hat look exactly like the type worn by whoever was in your hotel, as evidenced by the security footage your colleagues have now recorded.

- If you take the laptop to forensics for them to hack, add five minutes and turn to section 43.
- If you try and guess the password Webb would have used, if this is his, turn to section 135.

⋆ 272

"Mr Helsh, where were you the night of the murder?" It was a standard question, something you'd ask all people of interest in a murder case, and sometimes it produced a very bad reaction. This was one of those times.
"You're not pinning this on me!" Greg shouts. "No, no, you said it was questions about the murder!"
"If we could speak calmly Greg, that is a question I'm asking everyone in this room and a good few people beyond. Perfectly innocent, helps us complete our picture. Asking is in no way a reflection of how the investigation is going. Okay?"
"You sure? Why should I trust you?"
"An alibi rules people out. So, give us your alibi, everything's safe."
"Yeah, yeah I see."
A pause.
"I still want you to answer it," you add.
"Oh, right. Do I need a lawyer? Is this a lawyer sort of thing?"
"Most people don't need a lawyer to give us an honest answer to what they were doing at a certain time."

"Hmmm. I suppose not answering makes me look more guilty. I mean a little guilty. Yunno what I mean."
"That's not for me to say, Greg."

Turn to section 132.

273

"Do you have any further ideas on the Path killings?" you ask Greg.
"Well it ain't me, and I really want you to believe that Inspector, cos I bet everyone's pointing a finger my way, saying of that Greg, he's a nutter, but it ain't me and I got the alibi this time to prove it. And for anyone else...
Baxter reckons it's no one connected to the Panda, but why wouldn't it be someone connected to the Panda? Know what I'm saying? Still, I'd like to solve it and see this nutter take a pop at me, perhaps I should stick a blog post up and say I'm twenty-four hours away! That would be a turn up Inspector, that would solve your case! Me swinging and bringing the killer in!"
"Please don't do that Mr Helsh."
"Shame."

To ask if he knew Phyllis Wright, turn to section 246.
To ask what they were doing at the time of the murder / arson, turn to section 24.
To ask if they knew any connection between Phyllis and The Path, turn to section 97.
Or return to section 218.

You're beckoned over to a corner of the office, where Stewart has a brown file in her hand. She holds it up as she begins explaining. "Could just be a co-incidence, really could, but yesterday Toby Olney was released from prison."

"You're going to have to remind me," you reply. You know you didn't work on any cases with Olney yourself, but you can't remember what other officers had done. "Interesting character. Just served sixteen years in prison for attempted murder, using a carving knife he took from his mother's flat. Now, could be nothing at all, but might be worth us paying him a visit to see if he's got an alibi or anything..."

You nod and ponder, taking the file and looking through it. It wasn't unusual in cases to look for known criminals who might be responsible for an act, and you're within your rights to go have a quick word with Olney... who committed an extremely violent assault of just the same sort... but it might just be a waste of time.

If you go and speak to Olney, turn to section 194.
If you wish to pursue another option, turn back to section 100, you can always change your mind.

You look at the report of the search and lay in on your desk. Soon it will be filed away, and you hope you're never forced to look at it again. You're forced to conclude that Abraham Dealve is wasting your time, and he's wasted a considerable amount of it. There are people who, for whatever reason, insert themselves into police investigations, and spotting them isn't always easy. Perhaps, you say to yourself as you think of how resources have been distracted from the real Path killer, the fact all Dealve could come up with for a motive was randomly killing people you believe are connected as a warning sign.

But you checked, you were thorough, and you've given Dealve a caution for what he did. He's also been logged, so everything he says to the police in the future will be seen through the prism of trying to claim three murders and inventing two more.

You could do with taking a rest and recharging, but you can't afford anymore lost time. Instead you must go back to your previous leads.

Turn to section 46 to continue the investigation.

276

"Does the app business keep you afloat, financially?"
"Doesn't matter does it, wife's going to take half of that."
"You're married?"
Greg looks genuinely upset as he says, "Was. Am. Was. She left me over it all, the bitch. Dunno why she turned on me, you're through thick and thin, married couples, yeah, and she left me to rot, the sl... she ruined my life. For no reason. A man has a few problems, throws a few fists, and a marriage ends. Fucking hell. What a state. And I was the only one of the Cartel to be fucking married!"
"My condolences," you add, not knowing if that's the right word at all. "Can I just clarify something, when you say, throw a few fists..."
"What?"

"Are you just referring to the incident at the Escape Room?"

"What are you implying?"

"Did you ever hit your wife?"

Greg goes bright scarlet and bellows, "Ask me that again and I'll call my fucking lawyer!" Which, you have to note in your book, isn't the world's most effective denial.

"Where's your wife now?"

"Dunno," he says, avoiding your gaze. "Can we stick to the murder please."

You make a note and move on.

Turn back to section 166.

⌃ 277

As you walk briskly back into reception the man behind the desk sits back up straight and asks, "Did you forget something? Did you want a taxi instead?"

"Nothing so benign. I think the person who went into my room is outside, I'd like you to start looking at your cameras while I ring the police." You pull your phone out and make a quick call and are told uniform will send a car round as soon as possible. By then the hotel manager has appeared.

"What's happening?" he asks you.

"Someone is outside. Can we look at your cameras while uniform come?"

"We could but I can tell you we only have the entrance into reception and the vehicle entrance into the car park covered."

"What?"

"We use it to fine people who park too long. We log all vehicles which enter and leave... we don't monitor people walking through."

You suppress a long sigh and turn to look out of the glass doorway you've just walked in from. The urge to go out and search is strong, but you're sure you've done the sensible thing by waiting here. Uniform shouldn't be long; you are central after all...

Turn to section 122.

278

You lean forward and ask, "You said facts 'we hadn't already come to'. Do you share your workings with the rest of the Cartel?"

"Never!" he spits loudly, then regains some calm. "What I mean is, we do not share anything or pool resources, until we know the others have found the same, and then we will jointly confer as the secret is already out. I must remind you, Inspector, that this is a great challenge with a huge prize and none of the Cartel wish to see the others get it. Friendly rivalry, but rivalry all the same.

"What are your views on the others in the Cartel?"

Hewitt sneers as he says, "They would quite possibly need the help of someone like Hewitt, but I do not. They're all good puzzlers, or they wouldn't fit into our group, but they are not good enough for this as evidenced by the fact they haven't solved it."

"But you haven't solved it..."

"..." Hewitt looks at you like a cat observes a mouse with a gun before spluttering, "It takes time. It is a big challenge. I have complete faith I will solve it."

To ask about the puzzle, turn to section 258.
Return to section 267.

To ask about the puzzle, turn to section 258.
Return to section 267.

☞ 279

"Did you say Baxter had sent a message?" you ask
Robertson.
"Yes, as I was passing your desk, I noticed an email had
just arrived..." she replies.
"Just passing eh..."
"Well, you were engrossed, I might have taken a quick
peek to keep us all up to date," then she starts laughing
and shaking her head.
"Alright, let's see what Baxter has got for us."
 You click open on the email.

*Inspector. This is Baxter Hewitt. You said I may email if I
have any pertinent information. I believe Greg Helsh is
now a danger. He has made verbal threats about Mr
Forest and intends to hurt him to find the answer to The
Path. I was unable to record them, but I am now afraid for
my safety, hence only emailing. I fear Greg is the killer you
are after. He is violent. He will be violent. I fear he will kill
Forest. Stop him.*

You both finish the email eyes wide. First things first, and
you check the email address this has come from. It's not
spoofed, it's not fake. This is really Baxter. "We had
better go and find Greg quickly," you half say, half order.

Turn to section 206.

"We'd like to speak to Jason Weald please," you say to the Cartel, and a man stands up and walks over. With his tall thin frame, cheekbones, long tailored black coat and slicked back hair he looks like he should be playing in an eighties new romantic band rather than answering questions in a Sheffield pub.

"I'm Jay. Please, call me Jay, not one uses Jason anymore, not since my mum passed."

"Of course. What do you do, Jay?"

"I'm a full-time proofreader and editor, and a part-time developer of the Murder Wall. I'm forty-six years old and have always correctly filled in my income tax self-assessment forms." He sits down nervously, crosses and recrosses his legs, long coat being flipped about, and looks at you keenly, like a bird expecting its mother to instruct it on flight. "This isn't my first time in front of the police, I've been burgled a few times and have spoken then, although I guess I'm maybe a little bit of a suspect in this one?"

"No need to panic," you tell him, and begin.

◈ To ask, 'Did you know victim?' turn to section 10.
⁍ To ask, 'Were you at the meeting?' turn to section 92.
◈ To ask, 'Where were you the night of the murder?' turn to section 197.
◈ To ask, 'Was anyone angry at the first victim?' turn to section 25.
◂ To ask, 'Do you have any ideas about this murder?" turn to section 295.
◈ To ask, 'What's the Murder Wall?' turn to section 252.
To return to the Cartel, turn to section 212.

As you're reviewing forensic reports a movement catches the corner of your eye: the Local Mirror has updated. There's a new piece on The Path and the murders, but this one is specifically about The Path, and it contains a piece of your bait. Cross refencing this with your list of detectives reveals the person the bait was fed to: DC Wicks.

You go over to Robertson and explain everything you've done, and at first you can see in her eyes she's hurt and angry, albeit mostly the latter, but by the end she admits that yes, she too wouldn't be so keen to trust a constable she'd met so soon, especially as she'd known DC Wicks for a while, and it turns out they're the mole!

You call DC Wicks in and sit him down.

"Everything alright?" he asks.

"Do you know a journalist called Morton?"

"We all do, prowling around."

"And did you send him the briefing sheet I gave you today?"

"No! No, that's... that's..." you see him look at where he'd laid his phone on the desk. He goes to reach for it, but Robertson snatches it up.

"So if we examined your phone, we wouldn't find a communication like that?"

Wicks pauses, as if to assess the situation. He knows he's been caught and his shoulders slump down. "What happens now?" he says to the floor.

"You'll be suspended pending an investigation."

With the mole now silenced, return to section 129.

"Okay Robertson, what have you got for me?"
The detective holds up a piece of paper. "We've had a report in about a very angry landowner, very angry, you'd think someone had stolen something... and maybe they have. So, someone has been digging their land up. I think I can say farm actually, their farm up, he keeps finding holes being dug in it, crops trampled, that sort of thing. Of particular interest for us is the fact he chased someone off from doing it in the early hours of this morning..."
"So you're thinking if our killer found something out about the book, pinpointed an area, they might be digging to find the prize?"
"Exactly that, sir."
"Okay, we should speak more to the landowner, if we go and... you're looking at me and laughing. Why is that?"
"You know I said he was angry? He's actually come in and is waiting in reception."
You let yourself be led downstairs, and pacing back and forth muttering is a man in his fifties dressed in the full range of outdoorsman brands.
"Ah, officer, officer, some bugger keeps disturbing my crops!"
"Do you know exactly where the culprit was digging this morning?" you ask.
"Yes, I can take you right there now."
"I have a different idea," you muse out loud. "We could hide ourselves away and watch it."

❧ To monitor the dig site, add five minutes and turn to section 249.

To pursue a different course of action, turn to section 75.

"It's Baxter," you conclude out loud, and everyone turns and runs. You and Robertson dive into the car and head off, while uniform start the process of turning everyone to looking for Mr Hewitt.

As Robertson hits the sirens, she asks you, "Why?"

"He uses the same misspelling of Forrest / Forest as the letters the killer sent, and there's animal fur from a killer on Webb and Wright. He adores that cat and is covered in fur."

Then you have a thought and pull your phone. "He's not going to be at home. We know his MO, woods, industrial places, so the nearest one of those to the Forrest's house is, left here!"

You guide Robertson and soon slam your car to a halt alongside the car you know to be Hewitt's.

"It is him!" Robertson exclaims.

She calls headquarters to get everyone rerouted to search this brownfield industrial site, and you dash on through looking. Then a blur to your right, which you follow, and two people, oblivious to you.

"Where is it?" Baxter screams at a man kneeling and crying who you quickly realise is Forrest. "Where is the Panda?"

Baxter has a knife in his hand and is gesticulating wildly, but his focus is wholly on finding the solution, allowing you to come up behind him and strike first the knife hand with your extendable baton, and then Baxter himself. He falls, Robertson comes alongside you, and soon Hewitt is cuffed and sat on.

Congratulations Inspector, you have caught the killer. Award yourself fifty points and turn to section 95.

"As you regard yourself as the face of the Catan Cartel," you begin to Miss Krasinski, "how about telling me about the other members?"

"In what sense?"

"How do you see them?"

"See them... we're not a very tight-knit bunch, we wouldn't ring each other up for a heart to heart, but we are very competitive with each other. What I'd say is we are fierce opponents for the rest, but we respect each other too. I wouldn't look at the other three and doubt the skills of any of them. Iron sharpens iron and all that. I'm the leader of a good group. I guess I can go a bit further. Greg is just a big softy, you can push his buttons easily, and people who don't know him often do, but I know him. Baxter gets obsessed with games but it's tough to say whether anything comes close to his love of his cat. Maybe The Path has, but he treats her like a queen. Jay's a proofreader, and he isn't afraid to send your Christmas cards back with errors highlighted, but we still like him anyway. You've got to have a thing haven't, you, got to have a thing."

"What's yours?" you ask.

"Television. I've been told the camera loves me."

To ask more about The Path, turn to section 101.
To ask other questions, return to section 153.

"Can anyone corroborate that you were out running?"

"Corroborate…"

"Give you an alibi, say if you were running with someone…"

"I know what corroborate means, I'm just trying to think. I don't run with people, that would be a bore, I… oh yes!" He leaps out of his seat, "I track all my runs on the app on my phone! It will show you exactly where I was!" He stabs at his phone with a thin finger, and then thrusts it towards you.

It takes you a moment to understand what you're looking at, and you hold the phone so you and Robertson can look at it. You navigate a few menus and can only come to one conclusion.

"There's no runs listed for the night in question," you tell Jay.

"What? No, let me look again…" He urgently smashes a series of on-screen buttons, then sinks back into his chair. "I can't have had the app on. I'm always doing it. I swear I've lost all my record of my best time too over recent weeks. So the apps a loss then?"

"Yes."

"Then… I don't have any 'corroboration' to give you, I'm afraid."

You nod and make a note.

Return to section 280 to pursue other questions.

286

You open the book carefully, and find something very interesting… wait a minute, you're not supposed to be reading this section, there's no link to it in the book. Please don't read pages until you're sent to them, or you will spoil the mystery.

261

"And what, Mr Hewitt, does the puzzle mean to you?"

"I'm sorry, what?"

"You're clearly a dedicated follower..."

"Traveller."

"...traveller, very keen to complete The Path. Would what it mean to you to finish it?"

Hewitt sits with his mouth open, clearly reluctant to say the word that's come into his head. His eyes widen as he's obviously trying to think of the correct answer to tell a police officer, and you wait intrigued, before Hewitt evidently decides to just go with it. "Everything." He shuts his mouth, still wondering if that was right.

"Go on?"

"I mean, it's one thing to have a driving obsession with a puzzle, it's another to vocalise it, especially when someone's been murdered. But everyone in this room will tell you it's everything. We are all dedicated and have all spent hours on it. To not solve it now... that would be a failure. No one wants to be a failure. They really don't."

"In a way, you must like the puzzle, and Blanc?" You honestly don't know what he'll say to that.

"No. No sometimes I don't know if I do. But I must complete it first."

Go back to section 267 to continue questioning.

288

"Did you know Phyllis Wright?" you ask Jay.

"Isn't it obvious?" he answers, pointing to his face. "Phyllis was my psychiatrist. I saw her once a week and have done for the last five years. She's my rock, my anchor, the only thing that's kept me afloat. I can't believe someone's gone and killed her! I admit, I thought she'd had enough of me and was thinking of a polite way to move me on to someone else, and I couldn't bear that, but murder! It's tragic. It's awful. I can't cope."

"Why would she move you on?"

"I've not been responding to treatment, and she isn't the sort of psycho who'd string you along for money. If she can't help you, she's not seeing you. So, my days were numbered.

To ask what they were doing at the time of the murder / arson, turn to section 16.

To ask if they knew any connection between Phyllis and The Path, turn to section 86.

To ask if they have any further ideas on the case, turn to section 110.

Or return to section 46.

⌀ 289

"How did you know Mr Webb?"

"I guess you'd say we came into contact cos of The Path."

"What contact was that?"

"I knew his blog, right, and I read his blog, and socials because he follows The Path, but can I get in any trouble for this?" He still looks nervous.

"You can't get into trouble for giving us your assessment of a man."

"Yeah, good. So I knew of his blog, and I thought it would be good to invite him to come and speak to us. Yunno, we ask him questions and he asks us questions, a bit of networking, thought it would be a cool thing to do. But I regret it. Yeah, I regret it, cos he was a horrible man. He came to my house before the meeting, so I could take him, and he was rude, rude to me in my own house, but I gritted my teeth and I brought him along, but he was rude to all of us, just an unpleasant man and I wish he'd not come into my life. I should have picked him up by the neck and thrown him on to the next train back to where he'd come from. Awful, disrespectful roach."

Turn to section 49.

290

"I'm sorry Inspector, I don't know what's come over me," she says avoiding your eyeline.
"Would you like to tell me what you're doing?" you ask gently.
"I tried going for a drive to clear my head. You understand don't you, this murder investigation has put me under a lot of pressure, and the same for my husband. He's always been eccentric, but I have to be the sensible one and The Path was already a burden on us, but now I feel I always have to look over my shoulder for someone behind me with a blade, wanting to threaten me or similar for the answer. I'm beginning to wish my husband had never written this bloody Path... so I went for a drive, and I suppose I became lost in my thoughts as I don't remember what happened between leaving and now..."
"You were driving round in an endless loop, swerving about."
"Oh dear. Is that on camera?"

"Yes, it is."

"I'm sorry Inspector, I've not been drinking or the like, I should go home and not drive for a while, not drive until all this is over with."

"I think that's a good idea. We'll help you home, but we will have to give you a warning. This is not acceptable."

With Winnie safely home and chastened, turn back to section 129.

☞ 291

Unlike all the doors which are white and wooden, this one has been painted blue, and you're particularly interested in the small black box that seems to have been mounted on it. You knock, and within a few seconds a woman has opened the door. She's thirty to forty and is holding a brush in her hand.

"Hello? Can we make this quick, my paint is drying?"

"That depends, I'm afraid, I'm a detective in the local force..."

"Oh. Of course. Well don't worry it's just for fun, my painting, what can I help you with?"

"Did you know Mr Webb well?"

"The man opposite? Well, we knew to say hello and everything, but I don't know much I'm afraid. I don't know what he does for a living, but I do know he's very into some puzzle book."

"How so?"

"It's all he's spoken to me about for six months. Oh you know, you come out at the same time, say how are you, and he goes, 'I'm going to be rich, just got a puzzle to solve' and slowly, over weeks, you get a little more each accidental meeting and then... oh. Is he alright? A detective?"

"I'm afraid to say Mr Webb has died. I don't suppose that's a camera on your door, is it?"

"Yes, yes, it is..."

"And would it have been working last night?"

"You better come in, I have it all recorded to my phone."

Turn to section 200.

292

You have a private word with Robertson in Dealve's kitchen. "I'm certain he's making this up. That motive is gobbledegook, he's put no effort into it. There's no reports of anyone matching these missing men, we are a hundred per cent convinced the killings are Path related, Dealve didn't just randomly end up in a forest in my home patch. I propose cautioning him for wasting police time and getting back to the real investigation.

"Completely agree," Robertson replies.

You do as you intend, leaving Dealve behind shouting what about the other bodies, as you drive away and back to real work.

Return to section 46.

293

Jay is now refusing to meet your stare and keeps looking over his shoulder as if to see if anyone is going to come and help him. No one is, and none of the Cartel are even looking to notice his unease. "Are there many more questions?" he asks you.

"A few."

"If we could stick to the murder, please," he says, making you not want to stick to the murder.

"You write these yourself, do you?" you ask Jay.

"What?"

"I'm just wondering why you don't want to talk about this at all?" Jay seems on the verge of panic. "Is there something about the Murder Wall?"

"No, no, I just don't want to discuss my process, and if we carry on with this I will insist on a lawyer!"

"Okay Mr Weald, I can respect that. We will move on."

To ask, 'Did you know the victim?' turn to section 94.

To ask, 'Where were you the night of the murder?' turn to section 38.

To ask, 'Was anyone angry at the first victim?' turn to section 158.

To ask, 'Do you have any ideas about this murder?" turn to section 169.

To return to the Cartel, turn to section 212.

294

"Go on," Krasinski says to you.

"Sorry?"

"Go on, you want to do it."

"You'll have to clarify?"

"Like they do on the telly, go on ask, ask me 'where were you the night of the murder?"

"Yes, sometimes being a detective is like repeating lines from the box. Okay, where were you the night of the murder?"

"I was at home watching television all night. Might have heard someone say that line!"

"All night?"

"Yes, I was at school at my usual time, then had a meeting, so got home at 4:30 in the afternoon, settled in to do some prep, cooked dinner from 6:00 until 7:00, then watched the television to unwind. I know I'm not supposed to say this but, they may only be little children, but they can be incredibly difficult little people to deal with. To be honest, they're as rude as Webb was sometimes."

"I see," you reply, taking no side.

"I daresay some of these kids are more unruly than your criminals!" You doubt it, but you don't reply, which leads her to say, "Oh sorry, is that offensive? I suppose you deal with murderers; I suppose this is about a murderer. Those kids never killed anyone, although they would if they could."

Turn to section 61.

◄ 295

You ask Jay, "Do you have any thoughts on the murder?"

"I hadn't... I mean... " and he looks caught out, like a schoolboy who'd not done the homework, "I saw a report on the news, but I didn't start to puzzle it out or anything. Should I have done?"

"No reason to."

"I can only assume, if it's puzzle related like, you must think if you're here with us, what must have happened is he either solved it and someone killed him to silence him, or he fooled someone into thinking he was close, and they killed him for the same reason. Be a shame if he hadn't found the Panda, bragged, and got murdered."

"Would it not be a shame if he had found the Panda and was then killed?"

"Oh," and Jay looked even more guilty, "yes that does reflect back on me doesn't it."

"Do you think anyone in the group did it? Could do it?"

"No, to be honest I think they all had him lined up for press and coverage when they did find it. Even Greg would have given him a call and said get me and the Panda on your channel. We're a shameless lot, we really are.

Turn back to section 280.

296

"Caroline, where were you during the murder of Mrs Wright?"

"School. I teach, it was daytime, I have classes full of people who can corroborate all that, no problem about that one, no secret either. Definitely at school."

"I will have to place a call to find out if that's true," you tell her.

"Please do, in fact this is my headmistresses number," and as you get your phone out Caroline reels the digits off.

"Hello, is that the headmistress?" you ask.

"Yes, of Woods' School, who is this?"

"I'm a detective inspector working for the police, and I'm hoping you can confirm that Caroline Krasinski was working in class yesterday."

"I'm here!" Caroline calls out. "Everything is okay!"

"Of course, Inspector, I hope Caroline's not in trouble. Let me just check the staff sheet and... yes, in all lessons, no cover needed."

"Brilliant, thank you."

"Easy!" Caroline says, forgetting the weight on her shoulders for a moment.

To ask if she knew Phyllis Wright, turn to section 9.
To ask if they knew any connection between Phyllis and The Path, turn to section 146.
To ask if they have any further ideas on the case, turn to section 26.
Or return to section 218.

297

You don't tell the Forrests where you're going, but you happened to notice the location of the nearest newsagent on the drive in. When you see it again you note a largely concrete frontage on the outskirts of the 'old part', aligning perfectly with all the new builds for sales. There's adverts for ice creams and DVDs in the wide windows, and you step inside to find a series of aisles with barely enough room for you to walk down single file. A man stands behind a counter, counting through some scratch cards. To his right is another counter, a wall between them, and a bulletproof screen. The newsagent contains the local post office. The letters simply have to be handed across.

"Hello there," you say showing your badge, "can you answer a couple of questions for me please, quietly?"

"Sure, sure, how can I help?"

"Mrs Forrest."

He matter-of-factly replied "Yeah, yeah, she comes down here, buys her papers, gets her chocolate, yunno the score."

"I've spoken to her today, and she explained how she has her post delivered here, and then comes and collects it."

"Oh, right well if she told you, it's not a secret."

"Is it meant to be a secret?"

"Err... I kinda always assumed it was. Like. Yunno. Especially as she bins half of it the moment she sees it and takes the rest back with her.

Turn to section 217.

298

"What happened at the group, and what happened to make you regret meeting him?" you ask Greg.

"Arrogant. A really arrogant man, who thought he was better than us. Snooty. Yeah, snooty. Looking down his nose at us, all that. He only came to see if we'd tell him the answer, and I reckon that's the last time I organise a speaker or a guest or whatever."

"I know this sounds a daft question given what you just said," but you need to ask it anyway, "but did you have any contact with Webb after the meeting?"

"Nah, I put him on ignore. Everything on ignore. I would not allow him back to the group."

"He wanted to come?"

"I dunno I blocked him."

"Quite."

"I reckon he wouldn't though, not with..."

"With what?" you ask.

"With... what... happened..."

"And what did happen."

"You know, yeah, you know, you're trying to trap me."
"I assure you Greg, I really don't know. What happened that meant he wouldn't likely come back."
"Yeah, so," and he looks at the floor, "the guy was getting rude and disrespectful of me, and I stood up and shouted at him, and I'm a big guy, I got big lungs, and I got a bit angry, and I shouted at him."

Turn to section 81.

ꙮ 299

You stop what you're doing when your phone rings and you see it's from Sheffield's police force. Your heart sinks when, a few seconds after, DC Robertson also has her phone ring from a similar number.
"Hello?"
"Inspector, uniform have called something in you really need to see." You're given the details, and you and Robertson leap into her car and drive quickly through the city. You're soon stepping out into an abandoned industrial area that would be politely classified by the council as in need of regeneration. There's a long, tall fence along one wall, with a panel broken open so someone could get through. You've a feeling this is going to be important.
Two uniformed officers come over to you. The area has already been secured and SOCO has arrived and begun work.
"Hello detectives," one of uniform explains, "we've been investigating a murder that was called in today. Caucasian male, fifty or so, stabbed to death in this yard." He beckons to where a body is being photographed. It lays sprawled on the ground in a puddle of dried blood. The

face is twisted in fear and agony, long white hair and beard tinged with the rust.

"Jesus," Robertson exclaims, "someone's killed Gandalf."

"The killer was interrupted. We got a call from a club bouncer, passing through, who heard shouting and went to look. Attacker ran away, and the victim died shortly after."

"Description?"

"Nothing beyond hoody and jeans, focus was on helping the victim. When we came to ID the man, well, we thought of you right away."

"How so?" you ask.

"Body has no ID on it, but we traced it back through that hole in the fence to the hotel beyond. Nice hotel, and he was renting a room there, staff recognised him. ID in room gave us what we needed: he's Gareth Hyax, a fifty-four-year-old man and editor, sole writer and all around publisher of 'Puzzle! The magazine for puzzler's everywhere.'"

"Sorry what?"

"His last issue, which he was editing on the bed, is devoted to The Path."

Turn to section 62.

300

When the animal fur found on the victims is sent for DNA testing, it's revealed to belong to a cat, a match for Coco. As such, Baxter Hewitt is charged with three counts of murder and one of abduction. This isn't the first case where a pet's DNA has caught a killer, but it makes the top of the news even so. Hewitt is found guilty of all charges, having been so desperate to live up to his father he'd kill to solve The Path. He is unlikely ever to be released from prison.

If you have 70 points you have successfully completed this gamebook. However, if in this or other playthroughs you have acquired the following keywords, you may award yourself 10 points each. 100 points mean you have solved all the mysteries.

BREAK-IN
LOST
ORANGE

Well done, Inspector.

THE END

Afterword

I hope you've enjoyed this gamebook experience, I certainly had a lot of fun researching the format, and creating the story, and its characters.

Do you have what it takes to crack another case? Introducing: Crimescene Investigator

This outdoor murder-mystery event puts you at the centre of a crime scene investigation, and it's taking place in cities globally from 2024.

You'll explore the city streets guided by our award-winning mobile app. As you hunt for clues you'll visit different locations around the city, solve cryptic puzzles, and interrogate virtual witnesses.

You won't just be racing against the clock, you'll be competing against other teams to see who's got the best detective instincts.

Hundreds of thousands of people have already dressed up in their finest detective outfits. and now it's time to see for yourself why CSI is one of our most popular mysteries!

Find out more at www.cluedupp.com

SCAN ME

TIME CHART

(5)
10 ✓
15 ✓
20 ✓
25 ✓
30 ✓
35 ✓
40 ✓
45 ✓
50 ✓
55 ✓
60 ✓
65 ✓
70 ✓
75 ✓
80 ✓
85: turn immediately to section 299 ✓
90 ✓
95 ✓
100 ✓
105 ✓
110: ✓
115 ✓
120 ✓
125 ✓
130 ✓
135
140
145
150
155: turn immediately to section 187
160 ✓

165 ✓
170 ✓
175 ✓
180 ✓
185
190
195
200: turn immediately to section 162 ✓

GAME   BLUE
✓LAPTOP   GREEN
✓NIGHT
✓LETTERS
✓MAIL
✓ALPHA
✓SNEAK
   BREAK IN
   LOST
   SNOOKER

Printed in Great Britain
by Amazon

P188
50-7-46

(124)

"I'm afraid I do a lot of overtime..." you explain.

"Ah right, well, kids might have seen them. Yep, that's me."

"Do any of these apps relate to The Path?"

"Nah, that's a hobby for me, I love my puzzles but it's pure escapism from the stresses of real life. Yeah?"

"I imagine reviews and things online can be tough, you'd have to have a thick skin?"

"Lots of rude fuckers online, lots of rude fuckers, but with what's happened I don't care what some Subway employee in Wisconsin has to say about my stuff.

Turn to section 260.

⚜ 222

Scene of crime officers in white coveralls crawl over the scene, and the body of Phyllis White is taken away for an autopsy. Soon enough one of them is able to come over and give you a summary.

"Inspector, this was a frenzied attack. The victim was stabbed repeatedly in the front and in the side, with defence wounds on the arm and hands. The weapon was an eight-inch blade, which we have recovered from the bushes. It's a common kitchen knife, the sort you could buy in any supermarket, but it looks new. We've not found any prints on it, and the weapon wasn't cleaned so we suspect gloves were used. Gloves, in this weather? Sounds premeditated, that someone led her out here and killed her. In terms of all the evidence we can gather, it fits exactly with the modus operandi of the other two murders. I would have no hesitation in saying it's the same killer."